HITWOLF

Fred Adams Jr.

AIRSHIP 27 PRODUCTIONS

HITWOLF
© 2014 Fred Adams Jr.

Published by Airship 27 Productions
www.airship27.com
www.airship27hangar.com

Interior illustrations © 2014 Clayton Hinkle
Cover illustration © 2014 Ingrid Hardy

Editor: Ron Fortier
Associate Editor: Gordon Dymowski
Marketing and Promotions Manager: Michael Vance
Production and design by Rob Davis.

ISBN-13: 978-0692250839 (Airship 27)
ISBN-10: 0692250832

Printed in the United States of America

10 9 8 7 6 5 4 3 2 1

HITWOLF

Fred Adams Jr.

"All power is the same. Magic. Physical strength. Economic strength. Political strength. It all serves a single purpose—it gives its possessor a broader spectrum of choices. It creates alternative courses of action."
— Jim Butcher, *Proven Guilty*

"What makes a man dangerous has little to do with size, strength, training, speed, or weapons. Nothing makes him more dangerous than the simple will to kill. He'll always find a way to get the job done."
– John Slate

CHAPTER ONE
JULY, 1969

Tommy Cimino was sweating, although the night air was cool. He and Georgie and Vince were waiting in a shadowy alley between two grimy Newark tenements, waiting for the light to go on in a second floor window overhead, their signal that Laszlo Kovacks had come back to his apartment.

The illegal drug trade always has been, always will be, the ugliest of organized crimes in its execution, literal and figurative. Turf wars rival those of medieval warlords, and the methods of enforcement are largely unchanged, although by 1969 technology had moved beyond the thumbscrew and the rack. The old ways are still often the most effective; the message sent by inhuman savagery is one of warning, not only of surety of enforcement but of the unbridled aberrations of the enforcers.

The night before, someone had hit the mob's courier, Gino Canali and his two escorts, Rick Vallone and Hammy Porterro, and ran with fifty large. An anonymous tip led the mobsters to Kovacks, and Tommy was charged with bagging him and finding out where the money was stashed. Kovacks didn't just kill Gino and his escorts; he cut them apart, maybe with a chainsaw, and scattered chunks of them all over the office where they had waited to make the payoff. Tommy enjoyed hurting people as a rule, but Hammy was more than Tommy's friend and cohort, he was his cousin, and that made it doubly personal. This Polack would die slowly and hurting all the way.

The light came on in Kovacks' window just as the full moon began to creep over the cornice of the building next door. Tommy put his hand on the revolver in his shoulder holster and turned to Georgie and Vince. "Time to move." They stepped from the alley onto the sidewalk and the few people who saw the three burly men in suits averted their faces or ran the other way, if not knowing who they were, knowing what they were and that getting in their way was toying with death.

Tommy and his men moved quickly and quietly up the battered stairs to the second floor and the door to Kovacks' room. Tommy nodded to Georgie, whose size thirteen shoe splintered the doorjamb. The mobsters rushed, pistols drawn, into a dark room. They spread apart making three targets instead of one cluster and strained their eyes to make out shapes in the moonlight that leaked through the moth-eaten curtains.

"What's that smell?" Georgie whispered, almost gagging as he spoke. A rank, animal odor permeated the room, a cross between a wet dog and a toilet.

Through the open bathroom door, Tommy saw in the faint glow an old style ball-and-claw bathtub with an oval frame overhead for the shower curtain. The curtain was closed, and Tommy was pretty sure that was where they'd find Kovacks. He gestured Vince inside while Georgie covered the hallway door.

Vince yanked the curtain away.

Something big and dark and snarling exploded from the tub, bowling Vince over. Tommy managed to get one shot off before a sharp pain in his hand made him drop his .38. Georgie fired three more as the shape darted across the darkened room and crashed through the window.

"What the hell was that?" said Vince, pushing himself to his feet from between the tub and the sink.

"Goddamned dog," said Tommy. "Maybe a Doberman or a Mastiff; whatever it was it was big, and the son of a bitch bit me." He turned on the bathroom light and looked at his hand. The back his hand and his palm each had a horseshoe of bite marks welling blood. He stuck his hand under the tap and turned on the water. "Christ, that hurts."

Georgie looked through the broken window to the alley below. "Nothing down there I can see. I know I hit the bastard at least once, maybe twice, but that didn't slow him down much."

Tommy stared at his dripping hand. "Let's get out of here. The cops'll be here soon. Kovacks isn't here, and neither is the money. When I find that Polack, I'll cut pieces off him and make him eat them."

CHAPTER TWO

Full Moon over Newark. The cold light shone on a landscape from a post apocalyptic movie, an industrial wasteland of chemical dumps, abandoned factories and barbed wire with no one to keep out.

Crime boss Michael Monzo sat behind his desk in one of the cavernous, crumbling buildings. Through the grime coated window, he saw in the distance, beyond the airport, a postcard view of the Statue of Liberty and the magic skyline of New York City. The distant glow highlighted the profile of a face like a Roman statue, Julius Caesar or Caligula. Belying the factory's exterior, Monzo's office was clean, well-lit and comfortable; the furniture was expensive and the blue carpet lush. The tall, lean gangster picked a bit of lint from the lapel of his dark suit with manicured fingers and pulled a cigar case from an inside pocket.

Monzo clipped the end from the cigar and drew it across his nose. As he reached for his lighter, another howl echoed through the building. Most people would have felt the hairs rise on the backs of their necks, but not Monzo. He was getting used to it now, but his half-brother Eddie wasn't.

"I wish he'd shut up. That noise drives me nuts!" Eddie was pacing in front of the desk, nervously puffing on a cigarette. Monzo's little brother was, pure and simple, a thug. He was big, broad-shouldered, no-necked, and hairy-handed. His chest bulged out of his suit. "I'd like to go down there and put a bullet in his head right now and be done with it."

Monzo took a long, thoughtful pull on his cigar. He let the smoke drift out of the corners of his mouth. "Do you know why I'm on this side of the desk and you're on that side, Eddie?" Eddie stopped pacing and turned to face Monzo head-on. "Because where you see only liability, I see possibility."

Eddie shook his head and resumed pacing, and Monzo enjoyed his cigar, not ignoring the hellish howling from below, but calmly considering it, pondering how he could best use the odd gift that Fate had dropped in his lap.

"There's someone I need to see, Eddie." He wrote a name and an address on a slip of paper. "He is something of a specialist in dilemmas like ours." He handed the paper across the desk to Eddie. "Send Paco and the crew to pick him up and bring him back here. Kid gloves."

Eddie frowned. "Pittsburgh?" Monzo nodded. "And what kind of a name is Pegg?"

❖ ❖ ❖

The night before, Tommy Cimino and four others of Monzo's gang were waiting at the factory for a call to go after a shipment. They were killing time by playing poker in a downstairs room converted to a kind of lounge with sofas, a pool table, a television set and a fridge full of beer. Georgie was dealing, his coat draped over the back of his chair and a cigar in the corner of his mouth. "How many, Al?"

"Gimme three." Al Graziano was losing more than usual and he was getting pissed off. "Gimme three kings or I'll climb over the table and kick your fat ass."

Georgie laughed, almost a giggle. "Maybe if you shot me first. Tommy? How many?"

Cimino didn't answer. He started to twitch. His breath became short, his tongue lolling from his mouth. He began to sweat and yanked at his tie and collar, sending the button flying across the room. "Tommy, you okay?" Cimino's eyes rolled back in his head. Then he began to convulse and vomit blood, and he threw himself from his chair to the floor.

His buddies jumped from their chairs and backed away. They knew better than to get in the middle; Monzo had killed disloyal employees before, and at times he disciplined screw-ups the hard way as an example to others. Poison was not out of the question. Tommy's failure of the night before and the missing fifty grand were still on everyone's mind. Tommy screamed and rolled under the table, still thrashing violently. Then he suddenly stopped.

Graziano made the mistake of stooping down to look under the table. His scream was cut off along with his head, which rolled across the floor and bounced off the nearby wall. Then all hell broke loose.

The poker tale upended and the mobsters found themselves face to face with six feet of fur, fangs and paws like first-baseman's mitts ending in hooked claws. If it was Tommy, it was a Tommy nobody recognized. The beast opened its maw and howled, an ungodly keening sound, and in one bound leapt over the upset table. Georgie pulled a .38 from a shoulder holster and fired two shots, one hitting the creature full in the face. Its head snapped back, but it kept coming. The three gangsters ran for their lives and slammed the steel door to the windowless room behind them, locking Tommy in it and praying that the door held.

They saw enough horror films as kids to recognize a werewolf for what it was, but they still couldn't accept it as reality. Neither could Monzo until he arrived an hour later and looked through the mesh reinforced glass panel of the door. What he saw was evil incarnate that gave him chills, not at the raw, atavistic terror it instilled in him, but at the thought of how he could use the beast to instill that raw terror in others.

He watched in fascination rather than fright as the transformed Tommy rampaged around the room, howling like the lost soul that he was. He smashed what furniture was left intact, overturned the pool table with one impressive heave, and even leapt high enough into the air to shatter the overhead light fixture and plunge the room into darkness.

Jimmy switched on a flashlight and beamed it through the glass. Tommy was nowhere to be seen. Jimmy put his face against the steel webbed window to peer left and right. A blur of movement streaked from the left, and although the steel webbing in the port held back the paw, the claws erupted through the glass and ripped Jimmy's face. He staggered backward, blood streaming from his forehead, and a ruined eye dangling from its socket. Jimmy's screams rivaled Tommy's howls for volume and frisson.

"Jesus Christ!" shouted Eddie.

Monzo turned toward Eddie and said calmly, "No, I don't think he had anything to do with this situation."

Monzo's men pulled their guns but couldn't see inside the room to shoot. Beyond that common response, each reacted in a different way. "Son of a bitch!" yelled Georgie. Jimmy lay on the concrete clutching his face and blood streaming between his fingers. Paul started babbling: "It can't be real. Oh Mother of God, it can't be real." Eddie planted himself between his brother and the door.

Monzo knew that panic was contagious and had to be stopped. He slapped Paul hard, forehand and backhand and grabbed his chin. "Look at me, Paul! I said look at me!" The panic in Paul's eyes subsided. "Get your shit together. Understand me?" Monzo's grip tightened on Paul's face. "Understand me?" Paul gulped air and nodded. "Yes, sir. I'm sorry; I…" Monzo cut him off with a wave of his hand. "I got it. Now, do I have to bring somebody else down here, or are you going to do what I say?" They all nodded. Paul was calming down, but slowly. Monzo patted Paul's cheek. "All right; just keep this door shut and keep back from the window," and to Eddie, "Call the Doc for Jimmy." Inside, the beast's howls sounded as much like Jimmy's, cries of pain as of homicidal rage. Monzo said to Eddie, "Keep them away from the door and don't let anyone hurt Tommy."

Eddie stared with the same wide-eyed amazement at Monzo as he did a moment before at the monster. "What?"

"Nobody touches him 'til I say so."

"But Mike…he killed Al. He hurt Jimmy."

Monzo put a finger in Eddie's face. "Not one more word, Eddie. Do what I say." Monzo turned and walked away, leaving Eddie and the other gunmen, their mouths hanging open as he headed upstairs to his office.

Monzo spent the rest of the night at his desk with a bottle of scotch. The boys wanted to go in and shoot Tommy, but Monzo wasn't sure that would solve the problem. What little he knew about werewolves came from the Saturday matinees and the comic books of his childhood. If that information was correct, bullets would have little or no effect, and when the moon went down, Tommy would be Tommy again. The situation required only that Monzo be patient, something at which he excelled; wait and see what shape Tommy was in when he came back.

At 5:42 a.m., the moon set and the boys watching Tommy called upstairs. "Mr. Monzo, you should come down here."

Monzo looked through the door glass and saw a sweat-soaked Tommy, his clothes reduced to rags, lying on the floor on his side, glassy-eyed and panting. "Open the door."

The two thugs looked at each other and back to Monzo. They clearly didn't like the idea.

Ricky, a refrigerator-sized thug said nervously, "Boss, I…"

Monzo grabbed him by the throat and half-lifted him off the floor. "Ricky, when I say so, you do so," Monzo hissed through clenched teeth. "Now open the goddamned door." Monzo released his grip and Ricky reluctantly unlocked the steel door. "Follow me in," Monzo said over his shoulder. "I don't think you'll need them, but have your pieces ready."

Monzo stepped into the room, the mobsters behind him. The smell of flesh and blood was heavy. Gore spattered the walls and made the floor treacherously slippery. Graziano's organs were strewn haphazardly on the floor, his intestines draped over upended furniture. An arm lay in one corner; a foot still in its shoe lay in another. "Tommy." Monzo's voice was soft but commanding, an iron fist in a velvet glove. Tommy didn't move; his stare remained fixed on something far beyond the walls. A little louder. "Tommy." No response. "Tommy!" Monzo bellowed. He grabbed Tommy's ear and twisted it viciously. Tommy didn't cry out. Tommy didn't move. Tommy didn't blink. "Damn."

He stood up and turned to Eddie. "Tie him up, clean this place up and lock him in. I don't think he'll be any trouble, at least not until dark. I have to think about this for a while." He left Eddie, Ricky, and Paul staring at the wreckage of the room and the wreckage of Graziano's body and went back to his office and his scotch.

Certain things made sense. Monzo knew Tommy. Monzo saw what Tommy became and saw him after he was Tommy again. Monzo saw what Tommy did to Graziano. Monzo saw what Kovacks did to his men. It was no great intuitive leap to see the logical connections. He sat and smoked and thought and finally, having reached a decision, ordered breakfast and made a few phone calls.

That afternoon, Monzo read through books on magic and the supernatural that Eddie brought for him, those and an almanac. Moonrise was around 7:30 that night, and when the moon came up, Monzo was waiting at the door to what had become Tommy's cell. He watched mesmerized as Tommy transformed then once he was in full monster mode, Monzo went back upstairs. He'd seen the rest of the show already.

CHAPTER THREE

Pittsburgh, the North Shore; Tennet Street, little more than a back alley. Paco hated flying, but when the Boss said "go," you went. He and three of his crew took a flight on a chartered turbo prop from Newark to Pittsburgh a few hours earlier. The ride from the airport was almost as bad as the flight; the Penn-Lincoln Parkway was as rough as most of the Jersey roads for potholes and bad drivers. In a half hour they were in the city. Their driver rolled past the entrance to The Velvet Rainbow on Tennet Street, pointing it out to them before parking a block away.

The front of the club was painted in gaudy arches of color over the double-door entrance. The crowd that spilled over the edge of the sidewalk into the street was no less colorful. Goddamned hippies in bell bottom pants and tie-dyed caftans, sandals and peace sign medallions. They made Paco contemptuous and wary at the same time. Druggies were unpredictable, and that many in one place could pose a problem.

As the four of them walked from the car to the entrance, the crowd parted to let them pass. Frankie said in Paco's ear, "They think we're cops 'cause we're in suits."

"I don't like this," Paco said, "We stand out too much."

"Don't sweat it," Billy said. "I don't see three in the whole crowd I couldn't break over my knee."

They were stopped at the door by a gangly man in a flowered shirt and aviator glasses whose red ponytail reached almost to his waist. "Two dollars cover."

Frankie gave him a ten-dollar bill. "Keep the change. Use it for a haircut."

Inside a band called Prufrock was about to start a set. Paco turned to the doorman and said, "We're looking for a guy named Pegg. Where do we find him?"

Ponytail hesitated for a few seconds then pointed to a far corner of the dance floor. "See that crowd? He'll be in the middle of it."

Paco jerked his head and the hit men followed him through the packed dance floor as Prufrock launched into what seemed to the out-of-towners to be little more than rhythmic noise. People swayed to the music or maybe writhed was a better word. The hoods approached the gaggle of hippies in the corner and Paco saw that the people closest to Pegg weren't made of pipe cleaners and toothpicks. Four of them were well over six feet tall, and probably tipped the scale at two-fifty plus. They bulged bare-chested out of black leather vests and jackets. A few of their thick necks strained spiked collars. As the outside ring of hippies stepped aside for the suits, the big guys closed around a tall lean figure in a long leather coat, floppy hat and wire-rimmed dark glasses.

Paco shouted over the music, "I need to talk to Pegg." He looked over the shoulders of two of the bodyguards. "Is that you?"

Pegg smiled, the corners of his mouth forming an angular vee that accented the odd geometry of his face. The face that smiled at Paco was long with a sharp chin below a nose that pointed to it like an arrow. The eyes behind the glasses were deep set, and the forehead that hung over them like an outcropping of rock gave Pegg the profile of the Man in the Moon from the old bank calendars Paco used to see hanging in his grandmother's kitchen. He nodded. "I'm Pegg." He didn't raise his voice, but it somehow cut through the music and its words were perfectly clear as if he spoke inside Paco's head.

"Someone needs to see you. You'll have to come with us."

As if on a signal, Pegg's bodyguards reached into their coats, ready to pull. Behind him, Paco sensed his men struck the same pose. Paco raised both hands palms forward and fingers spread. Pegg raised an index finger in a holding gesture to his men.

"Where is it I would have to go to see this person?"

"Newark."

Pegg took off his glasses. His eyes slid to the side for a moment then back to Paco's, but his restraining finger never moved. For a moment Paco felt the dark eyes with almost no whites showing shine through his to the back of his skull. "I've never been to Newark. I'll come with you." He put spidery fingers on the shoulders of two of his men and they stepped aside. He turned to the bodyguard to his right, a colossus with a thick braid of white hair down his back, and said, "If you don't hear from me in six hours, you know what to do."

The bodyguard nodded, and drew back the lapel of his coat. Paco thought he'd be holding a gun. Instead, he was fingering an oddly shaped stone on a thong around his neck. The stone caught the swirling psychedelic lights of the club and shot them back into Paco's eyes. Paco tried to look at the stone, to determine its exact color or shape, but he found that it hurt his eyes too much to focus on it. Paco was glad to leave the Velvet Rainbow, glad to get back into the Lincoln Town Car and bounce up the godforsaken Parkway, and even glad to get back on the airplane to put some distance between him and Pittsburgh as quickly as possible.

❖ ❖ ❖

Pegg was silent and still on the flight to Newark. Paco thought he was asleep until Pegg turned his face, eyes closed, toward him and suddenly popped them open them to catch him staring. For an instant, Pegg held his gaze and Paco felt as if snakes were slithering around the convolutions of his brain. Suddenly released, Paco looked away. Pegg smiled, closed his eyes, and went back to thinking whatever it was that he was thinking.

Paco feared nothing, but Pegg made him nervous. For Paco, the plane couldn't land soon enough.

CHAPTER FOUR

They arrived at the factory at 2:30, the full moon shining through a rotting lace of wispy clouds. Eddie ushered Pegg into Monzo's office. He stopped at the threshold as if tasting the air rather than smelling it, then stepped inside. As he did, Tommy's howl echoed through the cavernous building. Pegg didn't blink.

Monzo gestured to a leather armchair facing his desk. "I'm Michael Monzo, Mr. Pegg. Please sit down."

Pegg nodded at the courtesy and as he sank into the seat, the howling began again. He smiled at Monzo and said, "I have an idea why you wished to see me."

❖ ❖ ❖

Downstairs, Tommy, in full monster mode, bounced off the walls of his cell like a fly in a bottle, howling and thrashing. "My problem is in there," Monzo said, pointing to the door. Pegg nodded and looked through the mesh window. As soon as the werewolf saw him, it stopped raging and fell into a crouch, as if recognizing a fellow predator. Its eyes blazed with hatred and a savage cunning, weighing the threat and how to deal with it.

Pegg put his face up to the steel mesh, which now bulged outward. Eddie shouted, "Hey, don't…" The werewolf leapt across the room, and thrust its fingers of death through the door. With the barest of effort, Pegg turned his head aside and dodged the hooked claws. Inside, the Tommy-thing howled in frustration.

Pegg stepped back from the door. "I understand your situation, and I believe I can help you."

Monzo nodded. "Let's go back upstairs and talk about it."

In the office, Pegg declined a cigar and a drink. "It would be indiscreet of me, Mr. Monzo, to ask exactly how you acquired your problem, but the problem exists, and I can tell you how to eliminate it."

Monzo studied the glowing tip of his cigar, took a drink of his scotch and spent a good minute considering his decision. "You misunderstand me, Mr. Pegg, I don't want to eliminate him."

Pegg's head tilted slightly and his eyebrows lifted slightly in curiosity. "No? Then what do you want?"

"I want a way to turn him from a liability to an asset. Given the right circumstances, I think he could be useful in my business."

Pegg smiled. "What a novel thought. You are a man of considerable depth, Mr. Monzo. I think I understand what you want, and I think I can accommodate you. I'll need thirty thousand dollars in cash and an airplane."

Monzo nodded. "Thirty grand and an airplane; that's your fee?"

"No that's what I need to deal with your problem. We will discuss my fee later."

Eddie's head snapped around. He snarled at Pegg, "Who do you think you're talkin' to, asshole? You don't just come in here and..." Eddie's bark was cut off by a simple gesture from Monzo, an index finger raised in an attitude eerily similar to that of Pegg with his underlings.

Monzo's eyes never left Pegg's. "Eddie, calm down and get him what he needs. Mr. Pegg and I are professionals and we understand each other. Neither of us could benefit by behaving badly. Isn't that right, Mr. Pegg?"

Pegg smiled again. "Indeed, Mr. Monzo."

Monzo returned the smile. "Do this for me, and I'll make you rich."

Pegg shrugged. "I'm already rich, but I love a challenge. By the way, tomorrow will likely be the last night he'll turn for the time being. I'll have to consult a lunar table to determine how quickly he'll turn again. It will vary between three and four nights most months, depending on how the phases fall. If you'll excuse me, I'd like to go back downstairs to study our problem."

Monzo pushed a button on the intercom. "Paco, come in here." In a moment, Paco stepped through the door. He looked first to Monzo then to the back of Pegg's head then to Monzo again. Paco raised a questioning eyebrow as his hand slid under his suit jacket. Monzo gave his head a short negative shake, and Paco frowned. Paco's gut told him to empty his gun in the back of the weirdo's head, but orders were orders.

"Paco, take Mr. Pegg back downstairs, and get him anything he may need."

Paco nodded. "Sure, Boss." Pegg stood and turned to meet Paco head on. Their eyes locked, and Paco felt the snakes in his head again. A cold drop of sweat rolled down his spine. At that moment Paco realized that Pegg knew what he was thinking, and that it was probably the last chance Paco would have to kill the bastard if it was ever a chance at all. Pegg nodded to Monzo and left the room, his long leather coat spreading behind him like an ebony cape.

Paco turned to Monzo, his eyes plaintive. Monzo, sensing Paco's anxiety, said, "Take him downstairs and stay with him. We'll talk later."

Paco took a deep breath, as if he were about to dive into a bottomless well. "Sure, Boss. Later." He swallowed his fear and followed Pegg.

Eddie broke a long silence. "Mike, that guy gives me the creeps. And it ain't just me. Paco ain't never been afraid of nothing, but this Pegg guy has him rattled. He's holding some cards we ain't seen yet. I don't trust him."

Monzo tilted his head back and looked at Eddie from the bottoms of his eyes. "I don't trust him the same way I would trust our father to catch me when I jump out of a tree or the same way you'd trust your woman not to shiv you any given night when you go to sleep. I trust him not to give me a reason to kill him. Right now we need him; maybe later we won't, but right now we do. And for what it's worth, Eddie, I'm not afraid of him but I know dangerous when I see it. He is dangerous, but not to us at the moment. Call it a calculated risk."

"This whole business makes my skin crawl," Eddie said, suppressing a shudder.

Monzo laughed. "Eddie, you're too Catholic."

CHAPTER FIVE

Before Pegg left for the airport, he consulted Monzo's almanac and told him, "One more night, and then he won't turn for three weeks."

Wherever it was that Pegg went, he was back late that afternoon. He entered Monzo's office with a wad of bills in one hand, and a small wooden box in the other. He laid the cash on Monzo's desk. "There's five thousand dollars there." He smiled. "I got us a bargain."

Monzo and Eddie stared first at the cash and then at the box. Pegg opened it and took out a small amulet approximately the size of a policeman's badge. "The moon will be up in an hour, and then we can see how well this will work." He handed the amulet to Monzo, who held it as if it were a live scorpion.

The amulet was heavy, cast silver. Its face consisted of twisted vines intertwined to form a rough hexagon. The vines were inscribed with runes that seemed to twist and writhe in the glow of the violet gemstone in its center.

Eddie piped up, "You spent twenty-five large of our cash on that thing? It damn well better work."

Pegg turned to Eddie with an indulgent smile one might bestow on a naïve child. "Among my associates, as among yours, the consequences for cheating are dire, perhaps even more so. I have every confidence, but you will be satisfied shortly when the moon rises."

Monzo handed back the amulet, glad to be rid of it. His palm itched where it touched his skin, and he shuddered involuntarily. "Now, about your fee…"

Pegg smiled again. "Perhaps not a fee but simply a favor when the time comes; if things work out as I believe they will, there will be plenty of time for that favor to reveal itself."

"I'd rather talk in terms of cash."

"Yes, I am sure you would, but as I said once before, I don't need money. However, as things develop, just as you need my unique services at the moment, I may someday need yours. We both know what a precarious grip anyone has on power, and what must sometimes be done to maintain it."

Monzo nodded, a little less wary. "Yes. That, I understand." But the words of the old blues song "The Ballad of Louie Alexander" teased at the back of his mind: "A gift from the Devil is a debt in the end."

❖ ❖ ❖

Moonrise.

Tommy was furry and furious. Earlier in the day the boys had dragged in a stereo system and now they played eight-track tapes of The Four Tops, Sam and Dave, The Temptations, and for variety, Tommy James and the Shondells to drown out Eddie's howling.

Tommy's transformation began as it did the previous nights, the shrieking and thrashing worse than ever. He raged around the room,

Monzo..held it as if it were a live scorpion.

slashing at the walls with his claws and clubbing at the door with his paws. Pegg looked into the room between thick steel bars that were welded that afternoon over the window. Tommy crouched as before, backing away snarling from the door, instinctively wary of a foe he didn't understand.

Pegg turned to Monzo. "Open the door."

Eddie's eyes bulged. "Are you nuts?"

Pegg smiled that indulgent smile again. "No, I am confident. Close it again after I am inside if you like, but I doubt that will be necessary."

Monzo's men looked to him, and the mobster nodded, part of him hoping that Pegg would be successful and part of him hoping Tommy would tear Pegg to pieces and he'd be rid of him.

The door swung outward, and Pegg stepped into the room. The door slammed behind him. Through the window, Monzo watched as Tommy edged cautiously around to his left and Pegg turned with him, facing him head on. Whatever mind rested in Tommy's deformed, elongated skull made its decision. He snarled and charged Pegg, arms spread wide. Pegg calmly raised the amulet in his left hand. He said something Monzo couldn't quite hear; something that sounded like the Latin the priests used to say when he was a kid. Tommy stopped in mid-stride and froze.

Pegg said something else in his foreign language, and Tommy dropped to the balls of his feet and the underside of his paws, forearms between his knees. His breath came in ragged pants, and the terror in his eyes told Monzo that Tommy was fighting this force with everything he had, but Pegg kept him under control.

"Come in, gentlemen." Pegg said to the gangsters outside. "I assure you it is quite safe." He walked over to Tommy, keeping the amulet in the werewolf's line of vision and put a hand on the beast's forehead. Pegg ruffled the fur on Tommy's scalp as if he were a child, and although his body didn't twitch, Tommy's red eyes darted back and forth as wildly as he had thrown himself around the cell minutes before. "There is no danger."

Monzo accepted Pegg's challenge. He opened the door, stepped into the cell, Eddie reluctantly following him, and stood beside Pegg. Monzo held his hand inches from a maw lined with vicious fangs and Tommy didn't budge. In a moment, he took the hand away and with Pegg, he and Eddie backed out of the room. Tommy remained still until the door closed, but as soon as the amulet was out of sight, Tommy roared and threw himself at the door so hard that it nearly came off its hinges.

Pegg's brow furrowed. "I had hoped that would have held him until he returned to human form." He looked at the amulet carefully then back into the cell. "We will see what happens when the moon sets."

Upstairs in the office, Monzo sat behind his desk, his fingers steepled. "So, Mr. Pegg, what went wrong?"

"Nothing specifically went 'wrong' as you put it, Mr. Monzo." Pegg removed his glasses and brought his eyes full bore on Monzo's. "Magic is not chemistry or physics; factors like personality, mental stability, intelligence, religious belief, and others insert themselves as variables into the situation. When Tommy reverts to human form, he is all but catatonic. It is possible that the physical trauma of the transformation, not to mention a complete division of his personality exceeded the limits of his mind. Those factors could affect his response to the amulet."

"But you still can control him, right?"

Pegg nodded slowly. "Yes, so long as I keep the amulet in his sight. You noticed that while it was visible he could not keep his eyes off it for more than a second or two. Besides, he will be human for at least three weeks after tonight, and we can make some plans and preparations to see how he might work, shall we say, offsite?"

Monzo nodded. "Tell me something, Mr. Pegg. One of my guys shot Tommy two nights ago, at least once. It didn't slow him down then, and when he turned back to human the next day, he was zoned out, but he didn't die from the bullet. What's that all about?"

"I suppose one of the perks, if you could call it that, of becoming a werewolf is that the transformation trauma is so radical that the body adapts and adjusts, healing itself rapidly to accommodate the changes. Injuries mend quickly as part of the transformation."

"So if we shoot him, it doesn't hurt him?"

"Probably no more than a wasp sting would hurt you or me."

"You talked earlier about eliminating Tommy. How does that work?"

Pegg smiled and laced his long fingers in his lap. "If you decide to eliminate him, I can make that happen, but at this point, that knowledge could be used in a moment of panic or anger and undo all of your plans and my effort. It may be safer if I keep it to myself for now."

"It won't leave this room," Monzo said.

Pegg's eyes drifted to Eddie and back to Monzo. "What was it Benjamin Franklin said? 'Three can keep a secret if two of them are dead?'"

"How about just one of them, wise ass?" Eddie's hand slid into his coat and his fingers curled around the braided handle of a blackjack.

Pegg ignored Eddie, choosing to look Monzo in the eye. He unlaced his fingers. "I can control Tommy." Pegg gestured with an upturned palm to Eddie. "Can you control him?"

Monzo's eyes never left Pegg. He thought for a moment. "Eddie, go get us coffee."

Eddie looked as if he'd been slapped. "Mike…"

"Now, Eddie."

Eddie stood up and stared first at his brother in disbelief then at Pegg with venomous resentment. He left the office without another word.

Once he was gone, Pegg continued, "I would suggest building more secure quarters for Tommy. Think in terms of a prison cell so that he is properly contained and so that we can more easily watch him, get a handle on his behavior."

Monzo broke in, "You're not talking about a cell; you're talking about a cage, like a zoo."

"Based on what I have seen when he's human, Tommy would not know the difference. In the meantime, you might also consider recruiting another subject who may be of sounder mind and body. We need someone not only skilled at killing but of the proper mindset; someone intelligent and stable. Once we have a better subject, we can more sensibly discuss eliminating Tommy." Pegg laid out a plan that seemed insane on its surface, but offered an internal logic to the whole mad scenario that made even the craziest ideas seem sensible. Pegg talked, Monzo nodded, and when Pegg finished, Monzo said, "I'll get my men on it right away."

Pegg sat back in the armchair, the leather of his long coat creaking against its arms. "Now, if I may, I think I will have that drink you offered me before." Monzo poured a scotch for them both and as Pegg raised his glass to Monzo, he returned the gesture, fully confident for the first time that he and Pegg were on the same team. He never could trust someone who wouldn't drink with him.

❖ ❖ ❖

Monzo took Pegg's first suggestion immediately. The next day, construction began at far corners of the basement, two cells with bars and steel doors; measures that would do a maximum security prison proud. When he was human, Tommy was no trouble, but Monzo saw what Tommy did as a werewolf, and took no chances that he might escape.

CHAPTER SIX

B efore the next full moon, a new problem erupted for the Monzo brothers. Two of their street dealers were murdered in separate incidents. Monzo's men were decapitated and their heads left sitting on their chests, the hit signature of Martin "Mardi Gras" Stubbs, Monzo's black counterpart in the Newark drug trade. Granted, their bodies were found South of Prospect Street, the unofficial boundary dividing Monzo's turf from Stubbs', but the killings violated a long-standing, albeit shaky truce between the two gangs and it was sure to bring unwanted attention from the Newark Police Department.

The next morning, Eddie was, as Monzo expected, ready to go to battle. "We can't take this lying down, Mike. I say we hit 'em and we hit 'em hard and fast."

Monzo thought this suggestion over for a minute and replied, "That's one way, Eddie, but it might not be the right way to handle this."

"That's what we gotta do; show 'em what happens when they mess with us."

"That's what someone wants us to do, but definitely not Stubbs."

Eddie blinked, "Huh?"

"Think, Eddie. Neither we nor Stubbs' gang have given each other trouble for a long time. Stubbs knows in an all-out war he wouldn't stand a chance against us. We have more men and more guns, plus we could bring reinforcements from the outside. And if they have to choose a side, the cops in this town will lean our way. Stubbs would have to be crazy to pick that kind of fight with us. We need to meet with him."

Eddie's jaw dropped. "Meet? What we need to do is shoot the frigging lawn jockey and hang him by his heels like Mussolini."

"We need to sound him out, Eddie. I think there may be another player in this game who wants us to fight Stubbs, and while we're distracted and played out, move on both of us and grab all the action. Maybe this business with Kovacks hitting our men is part of it. Maybe Kovacks is working for somebody who wants to take over and is setting us against each other."

Eddie pondered this a moment then raised his eyes to his brother. "I never thought of that."

"Like I said before, Eddie, that's why I'm on this side of the desk. Get Paco in here. "

Monzo was always good at watching two doors at once, but now he was watching three, Stubbs, Tommy and Pegg. The wizard, or sorcerer, or whatever he was nagged at the back of his mind. He understood Stubbs. That was all business. He at least knew what was working on Tommy, hard as it was to accept. He needed Pegg, but he found it hard to understand someone who didn't want money. If there was a fourth element in the game, Monzo's task was to bring them all together, like four spotlights center stage, to deal with all of them at once.

Two nights later, things got more complicated.

In a backroom behind a bar called the La-Ja 15, four of Stubbs' gang sat around a table counting money. The Motown thump of the bass from the jukebox pounded through the wall. Levon Bates stood guard outside, and inside, William "Mojo" Petty stood beside the door with a sawed-off shotgun. The mound of bills in the middle of the table looked like a minor haystack. From outside, muffled gunshots were followed by the splintering of the door. Mojo pulled up his shotgun, but was cut almost in half by machine gun fire through the outer wall. His finger jerked the triggers as he died, but both barrels sprayed the cracked linoleum floor.

Four masked gunmen stormed into the room, and emptied revolvers into the startled faces of Stubbs' men. While two of the intruders stood guard, one of the killers swept the money from the table into a duffel bag while the fourth pulled a meat cleaver from his coat and went to the corpse whose face was the least disfigured. He yanked down his lower jaw and with two practiced hacks of the cleaver left the corpse's mouth hanging wide in a grotesque silent scream. Cleaver Man then dipped a finger in the blood of the corpse and wrote a single Italian word on the table top: *vendetta*.

The door connecting the La-Ja with the back room was barred from the inside, forcing Stubbs' reinforcements to storm the place through the alley, where they met a hail of machine gun fire from the escaping killers. The bagman was hit, but as he staggered back into the doorway, a dark Cadillac, lights off, came roaring up the alley from behind Stubbs' men, running over two and scattering the others like bowling pins. It screeched to a halt at the alley door and the killers piled inside it. Gunfire starred the rear windshield's bullet proof glass as the hit men piled inside and the car sped away. The whole incident took five minutes and undid five years of an uneasy truce.

❖ ❖ ❖

"Tell me you had nothing to do with this." Monzo sat behind his desk, his hands curled into fists.

"I swear, Mike. I didn't do this or order it, and I wouldn't put it on without your say so. You know that." Since they were kids, Monzo could always tell when his brother was lying, but this time he wasn't so sure. This kind of shoot'em up was just how Eddie would react, both to Stubbs' threat and to what Eddie would saw as his demotion in favor of Pegg, the new player; maybe it was Eddie's way of asserting himself.

The word came from Donovan Brae, Monzo's attorney and the gang's intermediary with the Newark cops. Six of Stubbs' men dead in the La-Ja and one outside plus a few in the hospital, and the Monzo Gang's signature on the hit, the silent scream. That and the Italian word for revenge painted in blood pointed straight to them. The Newark P. D. was bracing itself for what it feared would be an all-out war and a firestorm from the press.

"Find out who did it, Eddie. If it was our people, find out which ones. If it was somebody outside, find out who it was. There's a pile of cash, a shot up car and at least one shot up guy someplace, and they won't be easy to hide for long Get on it."

Eddie left the office, and Monzo turned his chair to stare out the window at the late afternoon sun. More than anything in his crazy world, he wanted to find out who was interfering with his business before the rise of the next full moon, and he had only one day left to do it.

A knock: Paco. He stuck his head through the door. "Mr. Monzo, Pegg is back and said to tell you the search is over."

Monzo swiveled his chair slowly to face the door. "What did he say?"

"He said, 'Tell Mr. Monzo the search is over.'"

Monzo rose from his chair and for the first time in month he smiled. "Send him in."

CHAPTER SEVEN

John Slate was tired and hungry, but more than either, he was thirsty for a beer. Working construction was a good hiding place. So long as he kept to himself and did what he was told, nobody gave him grief or even noticed him much. The hard physical labor kept him in shape, but the repetitive tasks were mind-numbing. You can shovel only so many cubic yards of gravel or carry only so many sacks of concrete up a ladder on your shoulder before you long for a challenge.

Slate punched his time card and headed south on 14th Street, one of Newark's many seedy neighborhoods slipping into slumhood. Leo's, a nasty little bar festered between a small grocery store and a fire-gutted tenement building patiently waiting for the wrecking ball. Leo's façade was ivory brick coated with a generation of smokestack grime and street grit, its one window onto the sidewalk almost opaque. Overhead, a neon sign that buzzed like a beehive was missing the letter E.

L_o's. Slate grinned. If Leo knew what "lo" meant in Vietnamese, he'd either fix the sign or change the name. The door was made of thick oak timbers, with a barred window at face height. The old brass handle and latch combo was the only shining feature of the whole place, polished by an endless parade of thirsty hands.

Inside, Leo's maintained the perpetual twilight of dive bars everywhere. Welcome to dreamland, where you can park your cares on the sidewalk and for a quarter a draft, slip into whatever degree of oblivion suits you. Unlike so many bars Slate had seen, when the door opened, nobody's head among the dozen or so customers turned to see who was coming in. Nobody in Leo's was afraid of anyone in particular; everyone in the place was tough as nails, and they all respected each other's two feet of privacy.

Slate found a stool at the end of the bar with no hat on it, the local sign of occupancy, and ordered a draft. He emptied his pocket change onto the bar and settled into his own space. On the other side of the bar, Slate saw himself staring back from a mirrored Budweiser sign. Longer hair, a short mustache and a pair of heavy framed glasses with no prescription in the lenses changed his looks enough from his former self that even the Company's pros would have a tough time spotting him, if they knew where to look. The giveaway on Slate was a scar over his right eye socket that split his eyebrow, but he kept that colored in with an eyebrow pencil and covered by the glasses.

The worst thing about being a merc, a mercenary, is that when things go wrong, you are the perfect patsy for plausible deniability by the folks who hired you to do what they aren't allowed to do themselves. The Company had dropped Slate and his crew over the border into a tin-pot country called Laos to do some damage to what the locals called Trường Sơn but the pentagon named the Ho Chi Minh Trail in honor of North Viet Nam's Commie dictator.

Blow up some bridges, landslide some difficult trails, and generally disrupt the trunk line for supplies, manpower, and Communism from North Viet Nam around the DMZ and into the South. That was the team mission, until somebody told somebody who told some reporter what they were doing outside the designated theater of operations. Running American covert ops in a non-warring country was a big no-no, and once the press smelled Nixon's blood, Slate's team, and probably a few others like it were declared a liability and left to twist in the wind in hostile territory.

Because they were good enough, four of the six escaped Laos alive and scattered throughout Southeast Asia and, Slate hoped, all made it back to the U.S. in one piece. It had been almost six months since his team dispersed, and so far no one had opened communications. They were all believed to be dead, and the team was too big a threat to the White House and the CIA for them to come back to life. So, Slate waited. He was still alive and he figured his men were good enough to have made it back too. He could drop any of them in the middle of a jungle, a desert, or a battlefield anywhere in the world, and in two weeks the hard-assed bastard would come strolling into civilization with two hundred bucks in his pocket and a girl on each arm. In the meantime there was beer.

The street door opened and two men in suits came in along with a weird looking guy in a long leather coat. Slate watched their reflection in the mirrored Budweiser sign over the bar. They took a table near the back and pulled the chairs around so they all could watch the whole room. Dressed as they were, they were either cops or mobsters. Either way, Slate figured it was time to drink up and haul ass.

Before he had the chance, half a dozen hard cases busted through the door. They were all big, all street scarred, and all dressed in jeans and motorcycle jackets. The first one in the door grabbed a guy near the jukebox and spun him head first into the cigarette machine, a second sucker-punched a burly longshoreman who turned on his stool to see what was happening, and the fight was on.

The biker boys were pretty tough, and some of them brought pipes and chains to the battle, but Leo's crowd gave as good as they got. There were no allegiances here, but when outsiders crashed the party, they faced a united front. All Slate wanted to do was get out the door, front or back before the cops came. One of the bikers smashed a chair into a short, stocky trucker who fell backward into Slate, knocking him off balance against the bar. The biker stepped in to hit the trucker again, and Slate sprung from his awkward crouch to land a good kick with a steel toed boot that broke a few ribs. The heel of Slate's hand smashed the biker's nose and sent him to the floor where the trucker stomped on his face as blood spurted from his own nose. Around the room, the bikers bludgeoned the barflies and the barflies gave it back to them hard and vicious.

Slate's immediate objective, the back door, was fifty feet down the hallway past the johns. Slate ducked a punch from another one of the gang and caught his arm in the crook of his own, pinning it to his body and whipping around hard, snapping the arm at the elbow. One of the patrons rushed Slate with a broken bottle. The fight was turning into a free-for-all. Slate sidestepped the downward slash and kicked bottle-guy's his feet from under him. The man went down with a hard crack of his skull against the brass foot rail.

One of the patrons made the mistake of taking the fight to the suits, who, up until to then had sat watching from their ringside seats. As he ran headlong at their table, one of the hoods pulled a revolver and shot him in the chest. Slate heard the gunshot and doubled his effort to reach the exit. Turning his head, he saw a blur of movement and ducked as a chain whistled through his hair. The biker punk twirled it, a hopped-up glow in his eyes. He rushed Slate again, and as he swung the chain, Slate swung his forearm to meet it, letting it wrap around his wrist as he grabbed a handful of the links.

The punk yanked at the chain, and Slate feinted forward, throwing the biker off balance then pulling him back into reach. He let the biker's momentum compound the force of a boot heel driven into the bastard's face like a pile driver. As the biker went down, Slate looked toward the table. The suits were standing, guns drawn watching the room. The guy in the leather coat was calmly watching him.

Slate shucked the chain off his forearm and bolted down the hallway. As he ran, the rest room door swung open in his path, and he hit it like a linebacker, knocking the guy on the other side backwards into the stall. He rammed the panic bar full force and spilled out into the alley. Slate hit the ground running and picked up speed when he heard the wail of approaching sirens. The bartender must have called it in as soon as the fight started. At the end of the alley, he vaulted a chain link fence and dodged through the rubble of a vacant lot.

He needed to get back to his flop house as fast as he could; time to move on. His fake IDs were good enough to get him past a sidewalk cop-stop, but if the police picked him up, he could have some real trouble staying out of jail, and once he was inside, if the Feds sniffed him out, he might never see daylight again. He lost the fake glasses in the fight, and if somebody printed them and ran him through the Federal system, he'd be on top of the target list.

He slowed from a run to a quick walk, not wanting to attract attention, especially with cop cars cruising the neighborhood. Three blocks to the run-down building where he rented a room; three blocks to the bus station. Time to choose. He always carried his cash with him, and there was nothing in the room he couldn't replace at a Goodwill store. He turned at the corner and headed for a bus ticket out of town.

A block short of the station, a black car screeched to a halt beside him. He turned to run as the muzzle of a gun came out of the Continental's open window. No flash, no boom, just a quick "phut," and a bee sting pain in his neck, then Slate fell to the sidewalk, paralyzed. As he faded into blackness, he felt rough hands grab his arms and legs and throw him through the open back door of the Lincoln. Five seconds and it was done.

CHAPTER EIGHT

When Slate woke, he was lying on a cot, face up. He carefully opened one eyelid slightly, otherwise remaining perfectly still. He was alone. Slate was in the clothes he wore when he was tranked, but his right sleeve was torn off from the shoulder, and his wrist was bandaged tightly. A hint of blood seeped through the gauze. His feet were bare.

He turned his head and took a cursory look around him, ready to spring into attack at the first sign of an antagonist. He was alone in a twenty-by-twenty cell. Three sides were concrete block, fresh white paint, with one small window near the ceiling. The other wall was floor to ceiling steel bars. The only way in or out appeared to be a featureless door at one end. It too was steel. The cot was a simple steel platform bolted to the wall, no bedclothes, only a roll-up tick. A cast iron toilet and sink stood in one corner. Jail? It was night. No light shone through the window, and a harsh clear glass bulb burned in a recessed fixture in the ceiling ten feet overhead.

Slate rose to a sitting position. His head hurt behind his eyes, probably from the knockout drug. Otherwise, his mind and vision were clear. A quick inventory told him he was unharmed except for his wrist, which throbbed slightly. He had no ligature marks on his wrists or ankles. Either his captors were very confident in the drug they used, or they were very naive. Along with his shoes, his watch, his roll of cash, his belt and his Buck knife were gone. So was his wallet with the double thick Union card that hid a razor edged strip of surgical steel. No handy weapons.

The bars were substantial, spaced at four-inch intervals, too close to put his head through to get a good look to the sides, but what he could see head-on told him enough. Not jail. The cell was built in a warehouse or factory building big enough that the far walls were swallowed by the darkness. Slate clapped his hands and listened to the slap back echo; a big space and an empty one. This was no jail. And tranquilizer darts? A wave of anxiety shot through him. The Company found him.

As quickly as it rose, his frisson of worry subsided. He'd find out soon enough. He sat on the cot and waited.

Footsteps. Two pairs of feet. The door at the far end of the cage opened and Monzo strode in followed by the ever-present pit bull Eddie. Slate shifted on the cot to allow himself leverage to spring if either got close enough.

They stopped just inside the door, too far for a surprise assault. Monzo smiled and reached into his pocket for a cigar. He took his time to unwrap it, sniffing its length, and wetting the end with his tongue. He lit it carefully and blew a cloud of fragrant smoke. Slate sat through this bit of theater perfectly quiet and perfectly still.

"So, Mr. Slate, at least that's the name you're currently using, I have to congratulate you. You are a true enigma. You seem to have a name but no identity. My people are very good and very thorough. We understand what you are, but we can't seem to get a handle on exactly who you are. But Slate will do for the moment. "My name is Michael Monzo, he said, studying the glowing end of his cigar. "And that's no alias. Unlike you, I don't need one."

Slate appraised his captor. "You're not FBI or CIA," Slate said. "The suit's too expensive. And the cops don't drive Lincoln Continentals."

"Very perceptive. And if I were NSA, I suspect I would know all about you already. But yes, I am, you could say, a private businessman."

"And with chimpanzees like him following you around," Slate pushed his chin at the glowering Eddie, "I'm guessing Mob." Eddie bristled.

Monzo smiled in amusement. "You have demonstrated certain skills that I would find useful, Mr. Slate. Of course, I realize that you require reasons to ply them for me. And I will supply those reasons in good time."

"Piss off, pal."

"You don't talk to Mike Monzo like that," Eddie snarled. Slate leapt to his feet in a blink and Eddie's hand darted into his coat. Slate saw what he needed to see, the braided handle of a blackjack just above the bulge of a holster. Eddie was right-handed and carried his weapons under his left arm.

"Why don't you pull your nose out of his ass and come over here and try to stop me?"

Eddie took a step forward and Monzo raised a hand in front of hzim, halting his progress. Monzo spoke, never taking his eyes off Slate. "Don't be foolish, Eddie. He's trying to provoke you so you will come close enough that he can take your weapons away from you and use them on us both." Then to Slate, "I'll come back tomorrow, and after the night is over, you may be more interested in discussion."

The door opened, and the pair backed out of the cage. Monzo paused just before leaving. "If I send a doctor to change the dressing on your wrist, will you let him do his job without hurting him? I don't think either of us wants that wrist infected." Slate stared at him unspeaking. Monzo smiled again and slipped through the doorway. The door clanged shut, and Slate was alone.

The wrist was a mystery. The bandage was light gauze, tightly wrapped and tied in an old field dressing style by tearing six inches of the bandage lengthwise and tying the tails around his wrist. No pins, no hooks, no metal. He wanted to know what was under the bandage, but decided to not disturb it. The doctor was coming and he was going nowhere in the meantime.

Although his watch was gone, Slate had a good sense of time and estimated a half hour passed before a small man carrying a black leather valise came shuffling up to the cell. He stopped three feet from the bars. One of Monzo's gorillas, a size 50 stuffed into a 48 suit, followed him holding a trank gun.

The little man said, "I'm Doctor Wilhelm, Mr. Slate. I'd like to change the dressing on your arm. Please put it through the bars all the way to your shoulder."

Slate took the doctor's measure in a glance. Short, small-boned to the point of frailty, balding and wearing trifocals; gin blossoms on his cheeks gave him away as an alcoholic. Slate could kill him in a heartbeat, but now wasn't the time. He moved slowly to the bars, no sudden moves, and put his arm between two of them. The thug behind the doctor leveled the dart gun at Slate's bicep.

Nobody spoke. The doctor used a pair of blunt nursing scissors to cut the ties of the gauze and quickly unwrapped Slate's wrist. He turned it over and back again, examining it carefully. The doctor stepped back and pulled a bottle and a wad of cotton from his bag. Slate smelled peroxide. Wilhelm swabbed the wounds and rewrapped the wrist. Slate counted the turns of the gauze and estimated thirty inches, maybe enough to braid into a garotte, and if he played it right, he'd have a chance to use it.

Wilhelm tore the bandage into tying tails and knotted it firmly. He stepped back from the bars. "That will do it. I'll be back to check on your wrist tomorrow." He and the man in the suit turned and walked out of

"I'd like to change the dressing on your arm."

Slate's line of vision. Slate drew his arm back into the cell and stared at the new dressing, wondering at what he'd seen under it, two semicircles of bite marks, one on the back of his wrist, one on the underside, too large for a human mouth.

❖ ❖ ❖

Upstairs in Monzo's office, the crime boss sat behind his desk. Eddie and Pegg sat in chairs facing him. "So," said Monzo, "You think he'll do better than Tommy?"

Pegg nodded. "Yes. I think we chose wisely. We're dealing with a trained killer, not just some tough guy. He's no stranger to pain, either. His scars show he's been in combat, and that he's been tortured by people who know the best methods. He may find the transformation less horrifying; in fact, he may learn to appreciate it." Pegg stretched and rose from his chair. "The moon will rise shortly. I'm going to the cell to observe. Would you care to join me?"

Monzo studied the glowing tip of his cigar. "Not this time. We'll let you be the only person he sees and associates with the—experience. We'll watch it on camera." He gestured to a small black and white television sitting on a nearby table.

Pegg nodded. "So far, he knows nothing of his condition. The shock and terror of his first transformation will take him completely unaware, and he should be receptive and grateful to anyone who can make sense of it. It should make him more pliable."

Monzo tilted back in his chair and blew a cloud of smoke at the ceiling. "If he doesn't crack like Tommy." He tilted his chair forward and leaned on his elbows on the desktop, steepling his fingers. He looked at Pegg across the desk. He spoke around the cigar. "Make it work, Pegg." Then to Eddie, "Turn on the TV."

CHAPTER NINE

Slate lay on his back on the cot, hands behind his head. Supper had come on a cart rolled up to the bars of the cell by a thug in suspenders a white shirt and a pulled down necktie. The man with the dart gun stood close behind him. He pushed the cart barely within reach of the cell so that Slate had to stretch through the bars to pull it closer.

No utensils, no bowls, no trays, just food spread on the cart's top shelf. He fed himself by reaching through the bars for two hamburgers, a handful of raw vegetables and a baked potato. He drank a paper carton of milk and coffee from a twelve ounce Styrofoam cup.

Slate was hungry and he enjoyed the meal. He'd weighed the possibility that the food was drugged, or worse, poisoned, but decided that his captors had gone to too much trouble to bring him here to kill him, and if they wanted him sensible to talk in the morning, they wouldn't dope him up, either.

When the food was done, he stood at the bars of the cell and waited for the suspendered goon, who stood at a distance the whole time watching him eat. Slate wanted to see how long his jailer would wait before coming closer to take the cart. He could understand keeping out of reach of a dangerous prisoner, but the guard seemed almost afraid to come within breathing distance, as if he had some contagious disease. But that couldn't be right; Wilhelm stood inches away to swab the bites and change the dressings and the hit man with him was right behind.

Slate took a step back and wrapped his fingers around the bars a foot above the cart. He smiled at the guard but said nothing. The guard moved hesitantly toward the cart watching Slate's eyes, not his hands and held his own at arm's length until his fingertips touched the top of the cart. He rolled it backward, still fearfully staring into Slate's eyes. Slate smiled again.

He wanted to build false confidence in the guard, hoping that when he came another time, the guard would get just a little bit closer, just close enough for Slate to throw himself against the bars and reach through them to grab him. Maybe tomorrow.

❖ ❖ ❖

In a few minutes, footsteps; this time a single pair of feet echoed through the empty building. The man in the long leather coat strolled across the front of the cell carrying a folding chair. Slate recognized him from the fight in Leo's. Pegg unfolded the chair and sat in front of Slate. He pulled an ornate gold watch on a chain from his breast pocket. He opened it, checked the time, and snapped it shut again.

Slate got up from the cot and stood at the bars. "So what time is it?"

Pegg smiled. "Show time."

❖ ❖ ❖

Moonrise.

Slate's skin began to itch, just a little bit here and there at first, then all over his body. He started scratching at it but stopped when pain began throbbing in his fingertips. His breath came in gasps. His pulse soared and hammered in his ears as dark spiky claws erupted from his fingers and toes. The itch of Slate's skin turned to exquisite pain as dark bristling hairs pushed through every pore like white hot needles, covering him in coarse fur. His jaw stretched and he felt thick, sharp fangs push through his gums alongside his teeth.

At different times in his career, Slate had been shot, stabbed, beaten, and even tortured by professionals, but none of that came even close to the agony he felt as his body rearranged itself from within, joints ripping apart and reforming in alien configurations, barely contained by swelling muscles and a hide stretched almost to bursting. Yes, hide was the word, for it was no longer human skin, but the pelt of a beast.

Slate bent double and vomited blood as his organs were disrupted. He thrashed on the floor of his cell, writhing in pain and no longer screaming but howling, a high keening sound that was answered by another like it from somewhere nearby. And outside the cell, Pegg lit a cigarette and watched the scene as other people might watch a film or a play. Upstairs, Monzo and Eddie watched the same scene from the video camera. Eddie looked away, but Monzo gazed in rapt wonder as Slate transformed. "Christ, Mike, turn it off."

His eyes never leaving the screen, Monzo said, "No, Eddie. Get used to it. This is our future."

Unlike Tommy, whose muscles ballooned over his shoulders almost forcing him into a crouch, Slate's body swelled and elongated more proportionately, enabling him to stand almost upright. Slate's musculature bulged without impairing movement; he seemed, simply put, a more efficient version of Tommy, maybe because he was in better shape. Where Tommy's head had drawn forward and flattened, Slate's face stretched forward into a pointed snout, but his skull remained domed. What made the difference was a mystery to Monzo, but the difference was real.

For Slate, the rest of that night passed in shades of red and black, in flaming rage and destructive lust. He bounced from the walls to the floor to the bars of his cell like a pinball. He howled in fury and frustration as he groped through the bars clawing for the life that sat just out of his reach so that he could rend it to shreds and scraps of tattered, bloody flesh. Pegg sat, dispassionate, and smoked and watched until Slate finally collapsed in heaving exhaustion on the floor of the cell. Pegg checked his watch: much longer than Tommy, he thought; something to be said for stamina. He stood, folded his chair and walked away.

CHAPTER TEN

Slate's return was less painful than the transformation, perhaps because things were going back to their natural places. He sat up dazed and disoriented. He turned his hand over in front of his face as if he'd never seen it before, grateful that it was wrapped in skin and not fur. His clothes were rags, their seams split, shreds hanging from him like Spanish moss. The kapok from the bed tick was strewn around the cell.

The food cart came, but Slate hung back, although he was ravenous. His mouth watered at the scent of bacon, hard-boiled eggs, hash browns, and coffee, but he was afraid the food was laced with the same drug that had made him hallucinate the night before; it must have been a hallucination. It was too terrifying to be real.

He stared at the cart and didn't move.

"It wasn't the food, you know." Slate turned to see Pegg strolling across the front of the bars. "Go ahead and eat. I imagine you're starved after last night."

"Who the hell are you?"

"My name is Pegg, Mr. Slate. I expect you have questions. I have answers, but go ahead and enjoy your breakfast while it's warm. Neither of us is leaving here any time soon." Pegg smiled. Slate could not only speak but think after the first transformation; very promising.

Slate eyed Pegg warily. "Here's one. What did you slip me last night? LSD?"

Pegg shook his head. "No drugs. What you experienced came from within, with a little help from that bite on your arm. By the way, you'll find it's all but healed. That's a benefit of your condition. Transformation is so disruptive that the body must compensate by healing rapidly."

"What are you, some kind of scientist?"

"No, Mr. Slate, I am a wizard, and you are a werewolf."

Slate didn't laugh. In fact, he didn't say anything for several minutes. Pegg waited, gauging Slate's response to shock upon shock. The coin was spinning in the air and could land either way. Slate wasn't catatonic like Tommy, but he could still turn into a gibbering idiot. Or if his mind was strong enough and quick enough, he would accept Pegg's revelation at face value and adapt to it. The moment was crucial.

Slate reached through the bars and picked a piece of bacon off the cart. He turned it in his hand, carefully inspecting it before he folded it and put it in his mouth. He chewed thoughtfully for a moment and looked Pegg in the eye and said, "So now what?"

❖ ❖ ❖

When the cart came with lunch, a set of oversized drawstring canvas pants and shirt came with the food. Slate was glad to be rid of his tattered work clothes because they gave off a rank animal scent, but the new outfit reminded him of the shapeless suit on the land-bound Creature from the Black Lagoon. What Pegg told Slate sounded crazy, but given what he experienced so far, it offered a perverse internal logic: if werewolves were real, and if he was a werewolf, it all made sense. He never believed in God per se, but he saw enough in the far corners of the planet to convince him that things existed he couldn't explain.

The uppermost thought in Slate's mind, as always, was survival followed by escape followed by payback. To avenge himself, Slate needed freedom, and to escape to freedom, he must first survive. And to survive, he had to eat. The lunch cart offered fruit, sandwiches, and vegetable soup in an oversized Styrofoam cup; still no utensils.

Pegg came back during lunch. "It's good that you're eating. You'll need your strength when the moon rises."

Slate stopped chewing. "Am I going to change again?"

Pegg sat down and crossed his legs, one hand gripping his ankle. "You will change tonight and tomorrow; usually no more than four times nor less than three every month when the moon is right."

Slate's mind raced. Again and again? He swallowed his bite and stared through the bars at Pegg thinking, what I wouldn't give right now for a knife to throw through the bastard's throat. He's sitting there talking about this like he's planning a picnic. "So what's the point of all this?"

"Terror, Mr. Slate, terror." Pegg paused to light a cigarette. He held it between his thumb and forefinger, cupped inside his hand, like the Frenchies Slate knew from Dien Bien Phu, or the cons in the yard at Leavenworth. "Mr. Monzo runs a very successful drug operation, more by fear than by force or bribery. Power through bribery is weak at best. It is the left hand of blackmail. Power by force is effective only so long as your force exceeds that of your rival and it can damage you as much as your enemies. True power is holding someone else's fear in your hand and showing it to him, and as Eric Hoffer once wrote, 'It is when power is wedded to chronic fear that it becomes formidable.' You have become the source of that fear. You have become the Boogeyman."

CHAPTER ELEVEN

That afternoon, Monzo had a visitor, Donovan Brae. Brae's suit cost as much as Monzo's and so did this briefcase, which was conspicuously absent. No papers to sign; that meant he was bearing a message. When he arrived, Paco and Eddie were sitting in the office.

Brae was tall and fair-haired, a lawyer right out of central casting. He was a partner to Frank Bonnaducci, a guy from the old neighborhood. Donovan took over Monzo's affairs when Frank had a stroke the year before. Monzo didn't trust him as much as he trusted Frank but Brae had never given him reason to feel otherwise. "Hello, Michael." He sat unbidden. "How's tricks?"

The phrase was code: clear the office. Something for Monzo's ears only.

"*Mezza mezza*, and you?"

"Rich and healthy today," he smiled showing the dazzling set of capped teeth that charmed juries into acquittal. "Tomorrow," he shrugged, palms upturned. "Who can say?"

Monzo nodded, and turned to Paco. "Paco, would you excuse us for a few minutes?"

Paco stood, nodded to the three and stalked out of the room without a word.

Brae's eyes slid to Eddie and back to Monzo. He raised an eyebrow.

Monzo leaned back in his chair. "If what you have to say to me is what I expect, Eddie needs to hear it too."

"As you like. I heard from Whelker today." Amos Whelker was Newark's Police Commissioner and on Monzo's pad for the past decade. Word from higher up the ladder; not good. "Just what the hell is going on between you and Stubbs? Whelker and the Chief can't sit by while a gang war flares up."

"Our hands are clean. Somebody hit two of our guys…"

"Stubbs."

"And somebody hit some of them. Not us. And we're not so sure it was Stubbs' guys that hit us."

The attorney's eyes narrowed. "Not Stubbs? If not Stubbs, then who? And if not you, then who did this?"

Monzo leaned forward in his chair. "I don't know yet. But it looks to me like somebody wants to start a war between Stubbs and me and while we're weak from fighting each other, step in and take over."

"And who is this mystery man?"

"I don't know, but somebody's got something going we can't see."

Brae considered the idea for a moment. "Michael, did you ever hear of the Law of Ockham's Razor?"

"What? Who's he?"

"A philosopher from a long time ago. He said the simplest explanation of any puzzle is most likely to be correct. Whelker thinks the same way. So do I. I can't go to Whelker and tell him that maybe some unknown entity is killing your people with Stubbs' signature and killing people with yours and expect him to let us sort it out. This shit means headlines, and headlines mean pressure on him. Whelker's word is put a lid on it now, or he can't guarantee what will happen next time. What are you doing about this?"

"Paco's contacted Stubbs. We're meeting tonight to try to stop this before it goes any further."

Brae said, "That's a good step. I'll do what I can from my end, but I can tell you now, that Whelker's getting a lot of heat from the press and from the Mayor's office over this, and he can only hold the dogs for so long before he has to start making arrests."

"That's what we pay him for."

"Money buys only so much, Michael. There are limits to everything." Brae stood. "I'll tell him about your suspicions and see where that might lead. It could send the heat in another direction for a day or two, but don't count on it solving the problem for you."

Once Brae left, Monzo turned to Eddie. "We meet with Stubbs tonight at one o'clock. We'll see what's what when we have him face-to-face. I have an idea. Get Pegg in here."

CHAPTER TWELVE

The rest of Slate's day was uneventful. Even working the mindless construction job would be better than lying on the steel bunk and waiting as each heartbeat, each breath, brought moonrise closer and with it transformation. If I survived it once, he reasoned, I'll survive it as many times as I have to. Sooner or later, he promised himself, I'll get my hands on Pegg. His death will be slow and painful.

That evening, Pegg and Monzo appeared with Eddie, Paco and one of the hitters, Vince in tow. Slate took his usual stance, hands on the bars. Pegg was blasé, as if he were going to the corner store for a pack of smokes,

Monzo was eager, hoping to see his plan work, and Eddie and Paco were openly tense. Vince was sweating.

"You okay with this, Vince?" Eddie said.

Vince nodded, breathing through his mouth. "Yeah, this spooky shit just makes me a little edgy. It could've been me and not Tommy, you know?"

Eddie and Paco traded glances and Eddie nodded at Vince's back. "Yeah, I know."

Slate stood, hands gripping the bars, wishing that one of them, any one of them would come within reach.

"It's almost moonrise, Mr. Slate," said Pegg. "In a few moments, you will become the beast again. But tonight, will be different." Pegg drew the amulet from his pocket and held it in his upturned palm. Slate tried to look at it, but the gleaming rays from the violet stone at its center hurt his eyes, like looking directly at the sun or at an arc welder. He had to avert his eyes and when he shut them, he saw a sharp-edged phosphorescence dancing behind his eyelids.

"It pains you to look at it now, but soon you won't be able to take your eyes off it." He turned to Monzo. "Just another minute."

Monzo took a cigar from his case and lit it. The hoods shuffled nervously. All of them saw Tommy change at least once, and some of them saw Slate in monster mode the night before. They'll just have to suck it up and get used to it, thought Monzo. Like it or not.

Moonrise.

Slate felt the prickling of his skin and the needles of pain as the thick animal hair sprouted from his pores. He reeled in agony, throwing himself to the floor as his bones and muscles rearranged themselves. He howled as his face elongated and his gums bristled with fangs, and suddenly the pain stopped as if a door had slammed on a punishing gust of wind. He opened his eyes and they were immediately transfixed by the amulet in Pegg's hand.

He continued to change, but now it felt natural, normal, as if his soul were coming home from exile in a hostile land. From somewhere else in the building, he heard the howl of a kindred entity, one who was not granted the peace of the violet radiance. Instead of raging, thrashing, roaring, he crouched calmly as Pegg approached the bars. Something tugged at the back of his savage brain: kill, maim, destroy. But so long as the purple glow of the amulet's gemstone shone through the bars, the Slate-wolf was powerless to act on his own will.

Pegg said something in a strange language the mobsters couldn't quite hear, as if his speech made sound, but the words slipped around their ears like quicksilver and escaped before they could be captured and remembered. Slate heard them clearly with his mind: Kneel before your master.

The werewolf knelt before the bars. Pegg held the amulet as before, and spoke again in words that were not quite words: Submit. Bow. The Slate-wolf bowed its head. Pegg reached his free hand through the bars and put it on the beast's forehead. Then came the true test. Pegg held the amulet behind his back, out of the werewolf's line of vision.

Inside Slate's head, a voice shouted as if from the bottom of a deep well, "Grab him! Kill him! Twist off his head! Drink his blood!" But no matter how hard he tried to move, the beast body refused his will.

Pegg turned to Monzo. "His mind is considerably stronger than Tommy's. He will do as I command, so long as I hold the amulet, whether he can see it or not."

Eddie blurted, "He'll do anything?"

Pegg smiled indulgently. "Would you like him to roll over? Play dead?"

Pegg stepped back from the bars. The gangsters as a group stared, incredulous at the submissive werewolf before them while not a hundred feet away, the Tommy-wolf howled and thrashed like a furred tornado around its cell. At that moment, Vince began to stammer. "My God, it's horrible. It's not natural. It's, it's…" Vince let out a shuddering "Aaauggh!" His hand darted into his coat, but Eddie grabbed it as it came out gripping an automatic. Eddie twisted the gun from Vince's hand, almost tearing off his finger in the process, and smashed him across the forehead with it. Vince went down on one knee and Eddie kicked him in the face sending him sprawling onto his back.

Monzo looked down at the hood and said casually, "Put him in the cell."

Vince struggled, screaming, as Eddie and Paco roughly hauled him to his feet and dragged him to the door of the cage. The Slate-wolf's head twitched at the sound of the door opening, but he heard the calm, commanding voice in his head say, "Be still." And he obeyed.

Eddie shoved Vince through the door and slammed it behind him. Vince cowered in a corner, whimpering, staring at the back of the kneeling werewolf.

Monzo stepped up to the bars of the cell. "Vince, you've done things you shouldn't. I know you've been skimming for a long time, and I don't blame anybody for stealing a little. But you've turned on us, Vince. You sicced Kovacks on Gino and the boys, didn't you? Who's he working for? What's behind all this?"

Vince continued to cower, but there was a sudden, almost imperceptible change in his manner. The game was up. He stopped whimpering. His hand crept for the holster at his ankle.

Monzo tipped his forehead and made a sweeping gesture to Pegg. The voice in Slate-wolf's head said: *Stand and turn. Face your prey.* Slate obeyed.

"Last chance to tell me, Vince."

Vince pulled a short barreled .38 from his ankle and snapped off three shots, not at the beast in front of him but at Monzo. The first two ricocheted off the bars. The second ricochet grazed Monzo's forehead. As Vince fired the third shot, Pegg's calm command was firm: Kill.

Slate sprung across the cell, swiping a paw left to right and ripping Vince's jaw from his skull, leaving it dangling by gristle and cartilage. Vince tried to scream, but no sound came from the frothing red ruin of his face. He turned the revolver on Slate. Before he could fire, Slate lunged forward, jaws snapping at Vince's torso and ripping his midsection open, burrowing his snout in the traitor's gory entrails. Slate's jaws clamped on Vince's spine and shook him back and forth. It felt natural to Slate; it felt good.

Outside the cell, Monzo wiped blood from his forehead and Pegg watched dispassionately while Paco and Eddie stared in horror, too shaken to avert their eyes.

Slate hurled Vince's savaged body across the cell and it struck the wall with the cracking of bones mixed with a splatter like wet laundry. The Slate-wolf howled, an ear-splitting sound that shook even Monzo. The voice in Slate's head said, "Sit. Be still." And Slate obeyed, though every fiber of him wanted to gorge itself on the fresh steaming meat of the kill.

Monzo turned to Pegg and said simply, "Impressive."

Upstairs, Monzo, Eddie, Paco, and Pegg sat in the office waiting for Wilhelm to arrive to dress Monzo's forehead. The repeated howls reverberated throughout the factory, one voice howled in triumph, one howled in frustrated hunger at the scent of blood.

"You were right about Vince," Monzo said to Eddie and Paco. "He surprised me though when he pulled the second piece. I thought he'd shoot Slate, but I guess he wanted to take me with him."

"So you think the panic was an act?" Eddie said. He had pretty much regained his composure by this time. He had seen plenty of men die violently, but never anything like Vince.

"Yeah. He quit being terrified once he saw we were on to him. It was an excuse. He snaps out, kills Slate, and says, 'Gee, I'm sorry, Mr. Monzo. I didn't mean to kill your pet wolf man. I just got scared.' It's too bad he died before we could make him talk. But I don't know that he would have knocked off Slate anyway. Bullets didn't do much to Tommy."

"Ordinary bullets," Pegg broke in. "May I see Vince's gun?"

"Which one?" Paco said, pulling both from his pockets.

"The automatic, please." Pegg thumbed the magazine release and it dropped into his palm. He pushed the top bullet free and turned it in his fingers, studying it carefully. He set it on Monzo's desk and pushed it toward him. "If I am not mistaken, the slug in that bullet is silver."

"I remember the old movies where people killed werewolves with silver bullets, but I thought all that was bunk."

"Silver is poison to the werewolf, but one shot would be a mere inconvenience, slow to heal. One by one, Pegg thumbed the shells from the magazine. They clattered and rolled across Monzo's desktop. "All silver-tipped; eight shots plus the round in the chamber could prove a different story altogether. It might not kill Slate, but it could disable him for a long time, and the healing would be agony." Pegg's gaze swept the room. "Gentlemen, we are dealing with a third party who not only knows what you have but ways to deal with it."

"But definitely not Stubbs."

"I don't know enough about Stubbs to make such a judgment, but it seems doubtful."

"Well, we'll find out soon enough. We're meeting with him at one. Get Slate ready to move."

CHAPTER THIRTEEN

On command, Slate knelt in the cell as Monzo's men sprayed Vince's gore from him with hoses. He remained on his knees, head down and quiet as Tommy's outraged howls reverberated through the darkened building like the wail of Doom.

"Clean up this mess while he's out of the cell," Eddie told the men with the hoses. He shouted across the building, "Bring in the van!"

The van, a white Ford Econoline, was hastily altered that afternoon by a chop shop team to separate driver and passenger seats from the cargo area with a tight grid of steel rebar. The interior handles were removed like the back seat of a police car so that it could be opened only from the outside. The walls, ceiling and floor were reinforced with steel plate, making a secure transport for a deadly cargo.

Monzo gestured toward the Slate-wolf with his cigar. "Load him up. We meet with Stubbs in an hour."

❖ ❖ ❖

The full moon bathed the dew wet baseball diamond in a silvery blue light, as if it had been coated with drops of mercury. At the appointed time, vehicles approached from opposing sides of the diamond; from Monzo's side, his Lincoln Town Car and the white van, from Stubbs' side, a Cadillac El Dorado and a Fleetwood. The cars pulled nose in on their respective sides of the pitcher's mound, bathing it in their headlights.

Monzo and Stubbs walked from behind their cars flanked by two men each. Eddie stood to Monzo's right and Paco to his left. Bodyguards dressed in pimp chic, floppy hats and long coats that likely hid sawed-off shotguns, followed Stubbs. Stubbs came dressed in a suit as tasteful as Monzo's, almost as if the pair shared a tailor. As he approached Monzo, he pushed up the brim of his white fedora and tipped his head back to look down his nose at Monzo and his men.

Stubbs spoke with an arrogant lilt to his voice, drawing out the last word of a sentence a beat too long. "You called this meeting, Monzo, so tell me what's on your mind."

"Somebody's playing us, Mr. Stubbs. They hit me, I think it's you. They hit you, you think it's me, and it isn't either of us. Somebody wants us to fight."

"You saying ain't your boys hit my place two nights ago?"

"On my mother's grave, Stubbs; on my mother's grave."

Stubbs cocked back his hat and tilted his head, looking skeptically at Monzo. He chuckled. "Yo momma." His face hardened. "What you think I oughta do about it?"

"We should watch each other's backs, not jump to hasty conclusions. Do you know a man named Kovacks?"

"Name rings a bell. Heard it on the street."

"My advice is to stay away from him."

Stubbs snorted. His lip curled with contempt. "That right? Your advice? Since when I take orders from you? We ain't afraid o' you Dagos."

"There, you are unfortunately misled in your thinking. Pegg!"

Behind the van, Pegg opened the rear doors and Slate dropped to the

Stubbs looked down his nose at Monzo.

ground in a crouch. With one bound Slate scampered over the roof of the van and landed in front of Stubbs. "Holy shit!" screamed one of Stubbs' men, whose hand went into his coat. Before he could pull his gun, Slate swung a paw that caught him by the shoulder, spinning him off his feet. He fell on his hands and knees, pulling his pistol as Slate charged him. Stubbs' bodyguard fired, once, twice, a third shot at point blank range and the monster kept coming. With one swipe, the clawed horror sent the pistol flying, along with several of the bodyguard's fingers. Stubbs' men were too startled to move. In an instant, the creature had the drug lord on the ground. It sat on Stubbs' chest, cradling his head in its paws.

The claw of each thumb hooked into the hollow of Stubbs' throat. He was too terrified to scream as he looked up into the hungry yellow eyes. A long string of drool, sparkling in the headlights, oozed from the corner of the beast's maw and landed on Stubbs' cheek, as if connecting their faces. A dark, wet pool spread between Stubbs' legs. Guns came out all around, but Stubbs' men were frozen, unsure what to do.

"I'd say right now I've got the upper hand, Mr. Stubbs," Monzo said in a cool voice. "Tell your men to put their hardware away."

Stubbs hesitated but croaked, "Put 'em away. Put 'em away now!" Stubbs' men put their guns back, and Monzo said, "Now, a gesture of good faith, my friend." He turned to his men. "Boys, put them away." Monzo's men did as they were told. "Pretty simple," said Monzo. "One word, and our furry friend tears off your head. We got you this time, Stubbs; we can do it again, and next time, our friend won't hesitate."

Stubbs' eyes bulged.

"Maybe now you'll listen to reason. Maybe now we can cooperate. Do we understand each other?"

"Yeah," Stubbs whispered hoarsely.

"Good," said Monzo. "Let's not trip over each other while we sort this out. Keep the lines of communication open. I hope another meeting like this one is unnecessary." He nodded to Pegg, who spoke a few quiet words, and Slate got off Stubbs and hauled him to his feet. Then almost as an afterthought, he picked Stubbs' hat off the pitcher's mound where it had fallen and put on his head, slightly askew. Slate leapt onto the hood of the van, darted over its roof and disappeared.

In a moment, Monzo and his men were gone, leaving Stubbs and his crew standing in the glare of their headlights wondering what the hell just happened.

❖ ❖ ❖

"You know I hate this hocus-pocus crap, Mike, but that was beautiful." Eddie's eyes gleamed with the excitement of a kid on a carnival ride. The look on Stubbs' face when that monster had him on the ground; he'll never give us shit again!"

"I hope you're right, Eddie," said Monzo, leaning back in his chair and staring out the window at the New York skyline against the bloody dawn. "But you know the old rhyme about 'red sky at morning.' I had to think long and hard about whether to kill Stubbs. I decided not to because I think it would play into whatever plans are working against us. I'm hoping Stubbs will keep his cool and play ball with us."

"Stubbs didn't know dick about werewolves. Slate took him completely by surprise, so now we know that Stubbs didn't load up Vince's gun with silver bullets. And I don't think the other side has bought him off...yet. But that's always a possibility."

Monzo steepled his fingers and looked back out the window. "That's an unfortunate part of a free country, Eddie, the freedom to sell out."

CHAPTER FOURTEEN

In his cell, the Slate-wolf sat on his bunk, paws in his lap, like a school boy outside the principal's office, although he did nothing wrong. To the contrary, he performed exactly to Pegg's and Monzo's expectations. Like a well-trained retriever that will fetch game in its mouth and never chew its flesh, Slate held Stubbs' life literally in his claws and didn't yield to the bloodlust of the wolf.

Moonset would occur a few minutes after sunrise. Pegg stepped in front of the cell's bars fingering the amulet.

The voice swirled in Slate's head: "Calm. Change comes soon. Rest."

As the transformation wracked Slate's body, the pain retreated to another place, and in a moment, it was over. Pegg stood outside the cell watching Slate. A little more than a week before, the Apollo 11 space mission successfully landed men on the Moon and a few days afterward brought them back alive. What if Slate were among them, thought Pegg with a smile. On the lunar surface, would he be in a perpetual bestial state? Food for thought.

Slate came to himself still sitting on the bunk. He blinked his eyes. He felt some dizziness, a slight nausea, but otherwise, he felt none of the physical discomfort he had the first time.

"Mr. Slate," Pegg said, "Please open your shirt."

Slate looked up and locked eyes with the wizard. He had the weird feeling that the wizard was looking into him through his eyes, felt the sensation of something alive and alien rummaging around his brain, but he fought to hold his stare. "Why?"

"What do you remember about last night?"

Slate didn't answer. But as he stared into the wizard's eyes, flashes of his wolf-being played before him like a badly spliced film unreeling through a projector. A baseball field, Stubbs on the ground, a hat.

"You were shot a few times last night at close range. We both need to see the extent of the damage. Aren't you even curious?"

Slate's memory showed him the black man with the pistol, the muzzle flash, and the pistol flying across the harsh cones of the headlights. He unbuttoned the loose canvas shirt and held it open. Pegg smiled. "See for yourself."

Slate looked down. He knew every scar on his body, and today there were three fresh ones, not quite healed, each the puckering circle of a gunshot wound.

"Excellent," said Pegg. "And do you remember Vince?"

Slate's mind played disjointed splashes of rending, slashing, and the glory of a hot-blooded kill. Still he didn't speak.

"I'm sure your transformation both ways was much less disturbing. Part of that is knowledge, and part is my helpful hand. If you cooperate, I will continue my assistance. If not," he shrugged his shoulders, "you already know what lies in store at the next moonrise." Pegg turned and strode away.

Slate's mind reeled. If that bastard could control his mind, how could he ever escape? Wait and watch, he thought. When the opportunity comes, and it always does, be ready.

CHAPTER FIFTEEN

Across town, Brae parked his car a block away from his destination and approached the brick townhouse on foot from the rear. He stepped through the gate and crossed a narrow yard framed with high stone walls as a pair of unchained mastiffs sat attentive, silent, but ready to spring at any provocation. He had been afraid to pass between them the first time he came to the place, and his employer's creepy butler, Mr. Smith came out to lead him past them and into the house. The memory still chilled him, and so did the tall, hunch-shouldered Mr. Smith, resplendent in a tailored brown suit that fit him remarkably well despite his deformity. Incongruous with the quality of the suit was its condition, shiny at the knees and elbows, and all but coated with a thin patina of grime, as if Smith never took it off.

"Charybdis and Scylla," Smith told Brae that first day in an oily voice with a faint Irish accent. "You know ?"

Brae nodded, a cold trickle of sweat ran into his eye. It stung, but he feared raising his hand to wipe it away. "The whirlpool and the monster; avoiding one puts you in the clutches of the other."

Smith rocked his hunched shoulders and his gangly arms swung back and forth from the elbows in a parody of a badly managed marionette. He sang, "If the right one don't get you then the left one will." He cackled at his own performance and took Brae by the shoulder, leading him down the sidewalk. "When you leave, I won't be coming out with you," he said, tilting his head and showing a rank of splayed teeth in a crooked grin. "You'll just have to manage on your faith and your nerve and your good behavior," he raised his furry brows, "Counselor."

Brae passed between the mastiffs many times since, and he always fought the urge to turn and run, thinking, this is the time they won't let me pass. This time was not that time. The dogs' heads turned in unison, following him with their eyes as he approached the rear stoop. The door opened before he could ring the bell, and the grinning Mr. Smith leered out at him.

"Right on time as always, Counselor. That's a virtue, you know. Himself is upstairs." He gestured grandly with one of his scarecrow arms. "After you, sir."

Brae knew the way through the downstairs of the townhouse to the oak staircase past old heavy furniture as dusty as Smith's suit. Then down the upper hallway to the shadowy room where his mysterious employer waited, the man he addressed as simply Mr. Greystone but in his thoughts he dubbed "The Whisperer." He called him that because when the man spoke, he was hardly audible to the ear, but the person whom he addressed heard every word.

Brae knocked at the heavy carved door, and from within came the sibilant, "Yesss. Come."

The room was large, perhaps a converted master bedroom, with stamped tin ceilings high enough to be indistinct in the gloom. A soft glow from a desk lamp cast the only light in the room, and deep shadows splayed behind the furniture. The Whisperer sat behind the desk, as always, his face a grey blur in the dim light. "Please sit down, Mr. Brae." A delicate hand, long-fingered and carefully manicured except for a long, dagger-shaped thumbnail, gestured to a single straight-backed chair.

Brae sat and knew to not speak until he has spoken to.

"What do you have to tell me today?"

Brae swallowed nervously. "Things are going slowly. Monzo is savvy enough to suspect a third party is trying to set him and Stubbs against each other." He hastily added, "But he has no idea of your identity."

"Did he mention problems among his," The Whisperer hesitated, searching for the word that pleased him, "...personnel?"

"No, he didn't."

"You are correct in your estimation of Mr. Monzo. He is indeed very savvy. Our operative in his ranks has not reported to me as scheduled, and I assume Mr. Monzo has discovered him and dispatched him, probably before he could carry out his orders."

"He didn't say anything about it to me. I tried to convince him that he was being a paranoid, but he's not buying it. He said, 'Somebody's got something going we can't see.'"

The Whisperer sat silent and unmoving for a full minute, thinking, weighing, deciding. Finally, he spoke. "Mr. Monzo is correct. Things are happening that he cannot see and that you have not seen up to now, but with the unfortunate Vincent eliminated, I need another ear in Monzo's camp. You will become that ear, and there are things I must explain so that you will understand what must be done and be done quickly."

Brae shifted uncomfortably in his chair. "Mr. Greystone, I don't think I can..."

The whisper became a hiss. "You can and you will. Did Monzo mention a man named Pegg?"

Brae shook his head quickly. "No, Mr. Greystone, no one by that name."

For the first time since Brae had met him, The Whisperer's voice betrayed his emotion: anger. "This man Pegg's introduction into the matrix has changed much. I must know how much and in what ways, and it is up to you to discover that for me and to take appropriate action. Am I clear?"

"Yes, but..."

"Now, tell me, Mr. Brae, what do you know about lycanthropy?"

For the next hour, The Whisperer dismantled Brae's entire sense of reality and rebuilt it in a skewed parody of all he ever believed. The

Whisperer outlined the plan behind the plan: sew chaos in Monzo's organization by infecting one of his inner circle with werewolfery in the hope that the infection would spread among his men and they would slaughter each other, perhaps even Monzo himself and bring down the gang lord. But Monzo was lucky and as Brae put it, savvy.

The Whisperer set a pale multifaceted gemstone the size of a fist in the circle of light on his desk and told Brae to look into it. "It will help you to understand what I have told you and am about to tell you, and it will show you things, shall we say, beyond the spoken word."

Brae looked into the stone, and as he stared, the edges of the facets began to undulate and shift, as if the stone were a beating heart and though he never left his chair, he felt himself drawn toward it. The stone seemed to swell enormously or rather he shrank and fell through its surface like a grain of sand into a glass of wine.

From outside the stone, the enormous hooded eyes of the Whisperer peered in at him as he might inspect an insect trapped in amber. The voice hissed and whistled through the convolutions of his brain. Every dread creature from his childhood nightmares, the things he was too terrified to remember upon waking, waited on the other side of the stone, leering in through one facet or another. The voice told him what he must do, and the drooling shapes ogling him told him what they would do if he failed. Brae fell to his knees to the floor. He squeezed his eyes shut and all but drove his thumbs through his eardrums to shut out their shrieks and moans. He passed out, and when he awoke moments later, he lay in a fetal curl in front of The Whisperer's desk.

"Stand." Brae felt the command more than he heard it. He used the chair to pull himself to his feet. "Give me your hand." Brae's fingers twitched as he reached into the pool of light on the desk. The Whisperer's left hand clamped onto Brae's wrist like a manacle, pinning it to the desk. The pointed nail of the Whisperer's thumb proved as sharp as a scalpel. It lightly traced a design on the back of Brae's hand and blood welled from the fine cuts.

The Whisperer released his grip and Brae stared at the odd sigil carved into his skin, a scalene triangle with two lines parallel to its base and a vertical line from its apex that reached beyond its boundaries. As he stared the blood and the cuts faded into his skin as if they were never there. "Now you are shielded. And you are mine.

"Mr. Smith." Instantly the door opened and Smith shuffled inside. "Show Mr. Brae out, please."

Smith genuflected and put a claw-like hand on Brae's arm, turning him toward the door. "This way, Counselor," he cackled. Brae swayed on his feet. He turned to look back at The Whisperer who said one word from his shadows: "Remember."

As the rear door closed behind him and Brae found himself once more in the sunlight, he felt a great relief, that is, until he looked down the narrow walk and saw Charybdis and Scylla snap to attention. He held his breath while he moved with mincing steps between the mastiffs as their heads turned, keeping him in their sight until he closed the alley gate and leaned against it, almost in a faint. My God, he thought, what have I gotten myself into?

Brae's hands shook so badly that he couldn't slide the key into his Mercedes' ignition for a full minute. When he was first approached to work for the Whisperer, it all seemed a simple matter of choosing of sides in a plot for wealth and power. Gradually over the course of the last six months Brae found himself sliding down a precipitous funnel of increasing illegality but nothing so bizarre and outrageous as the supernatural scenario The Whisperer laid before him.

If Monzo found him out, Brae would simply disappear, or his corpse would wash ashore on some stretch of the Passaic in a swirl of garbage, dead fish and used condoms. But that would not be the end. The Whisperer showed him his life in the stone and what waited for him beyond it if he failed. He could not afford to fail.

CHAPTER SIXTEEN

Slate was no stranger to imprisonment. The difference between him and the average prisoner was the training that made Slate more likely to escape. The worst of foreign jails and prison camps were no match for him, and he figured that his current accommodation couldn't hold him for long. But if he escaped, then what? He was trapped less by the bars than by the curse, or infection, or whatever it was. His lack of control over his situation bothered him the most. Pegg could control him with a word when he was in monster mode. Whatever he would do must be done while he was human, and he would be that for at least two more weeks.

Confinement gave Slate plenty of time to think, to evaluate his situation. Immediate escape was unlikely. He was stuck for the moment because until the next full moon he was of no concern. He was fed and bed-checked regularly, but otherwise ignored. They took him out of the cell once, he thought, and they'd do it again, but if that bastard Pegg kept the magic leash on him, he had little chance to get away.

Another nagging thought was the prisoner at the other end of the building. When he was in wolf mode, Slate could instinctively feel his presence, but he was silent the rest of the time. Who was he? Did Monzo shanghai him the same way he did Slate? Could he be an ally? Too many questions without immediate answers, and nobody would talk. *Omerta*, the code of silence was the rule of the day. All he could do was wait and watch.

As he lay on his bunk at night, slate thought more than once that if he could have changed into a werewolf on the Ho Chi Minh Trail, he probably would have scared the superstitious Viet Cong right out of their black pajamas and all the way back to Hanoi. If the CIA only knew. Yeah, Slate thought, if the CIA and the Pentagon weapons division and Hoover's FBI only knew, they'd be in a bureaucratic bitch slapping fight over him for the rest of his life.

The irony was that if Monzo wanted someone killed, or something torched, or something blown up, Slate was a merc. Monzo could simply have paid him and he'd probably have done it, and done it more efficiently than the gorillas on Monzo's payroll. Slate never killed for sport or for spite, but a job was a job. Abducting him and turning him into a werewolf made Slate his servant when the moon was full, but a wasted resource when it wasn't. Monzo was no fool, but if Slate dangled the right bait, he might get out of the cage just long enough to get away. Survive. Escape.

❖ ❖ ❖

A week after the full moon Slate decided to play the card. When one of Monzo's men, the tall, thick thug he'd heard someone call Georgie brought the food cart, Slate stepped up to the bars and called to him as he walked away.

"Hey Georgie!" Georgie stopped and turned but didn't answer. "Tell Mr. Monzo I'd like to talk to him. At his convenience, of course," Slate said with a chuckle. "I'll be here all day."

Georgie, still unspeaking, turned and walked away.

❖ ❖ ❖

A knock at Monzo's door. Eddie opened it to find Paco with Georgie. "Mr. Monzo, Georgie has something to tell you." Georgie followed Paco into the office with his cap in his hand, visibly nervous in the presence of the boss. He huddled his shoulders inward and bowed his head, as if trying to appear smaller than he was.

"Yes, Georgie," Monzo said, smiling; no offer of a seat, a drink or a cigar. "What is it you want to tell me?"

"Mr. Monzo, the guy in the cage..."

"Yes, Georgie. What about him?"

"He said to tell you he wants to talk to you."

Monzo's brow creased in thought. "Did he say anything else?"

"Yeah, he said at your convenience."

Monzo barked an unexpected laugh, surprising everyone in the room. "Thanks for telling me, Georgie. Now if you'll excuse me..."

Paco took Georgie by the elbow and steered him out the door. When it closed behind them, Monzo turned to Eddie and said, "He wants to talk to me. Not Pegg, me. Interesting."

"You gonna talk to him?"

"No, Eddie, just listen. I think he wants to make a deal. But let him wait a while. Let's remind him that I call the shots"

Slate enjoyed a leisurely lunch, stretched out on his cot, and waited all day, and the next, and the next. All he could do for the moment was watch and wait and learn. In the meantime, he occupied his mind by reading the paperbacked novels his captors brought in by the armload. He asked for a newspaper once, but Monzo, or Pegg, or whoever made such decisions wanted him completely isolated from the world at large. So they brought him novels instead. Among them he read the adventures of James Bond, Matt Helm, Harry Palmer, Quiller. Slate once found such novels absurd and unrealistic based on his field experience, but he found his current situation no less fantastic, and it was real. Fleming described James Bond's captivity in *Dr. No* as a "mink-lined prison." No mink here, thought Slate, but at least the food is good.

He occupied his body by driving it to the point of exhaustion with a daily exercise regimen. He did pushups, crunches, and squat thrusts until his muscles screamed, and then he did more. Without a horizontal bar for chinning, Slate did isometric curls against his bunk, finally working its bolts loose from the wall. One morning a hefty pair of cast iron dumbbells came with breakfast on the cart. They barely fit through the bars of the cell. One piece of solid iron each, they offered no parts he could disassemble to make a weapon, but they were useful to Slate's training.

Although he couldn't run, he was in better shape than he could remember. How much of it was food, sleep and exercise, and how much the mixed blessings of his affliction? No way to tell. He did *katas* too, sharpening his martial arts skills to a fine edge. No need to hide his skills. Monzo knew what he was, Slate realized, chose him for it, in fact. When opportunity opened the door, he wanted to be ready. His goal was to become as dangerous as a human as he was as a werewolf. If he were not already, Slate was well on his way. As Colonel Marsh, his mentor once told him, "When they take away their weapons, become one yourself."

They even sent a woman one night, a good looking red-headed hooker. She didn't fear him at all, and Slate figured they didn't warn her about him. She stood outside the cell and beckoned him to come to the bars. In spite of desire Slate kept his distance even when she pulled her dress over her head revealing her nakedness underneath and did a silent dance that would have seduced John the Baptist. Slate refused to put on a peep show for Monzo's goons, but something strange happened. In his moment of arousal, Slate felt the stirring of the change, just a shuddering hint, but the feeling was unmistakable. After she left, Slate pondered the implications.

Could strong emotions trigger the transformation? Slate felt absolute hatred for Monzo and murderous anger toward Pegg, but neither of those had made the blood tide rise inside him. Was sex a trigger, or could it be that the more often he changed the weaker the wall became between him and the beast?

Two weeks had passed since his last transformation. If Pegg told the truth, he had a week, more or less, before he became the beast again. Since he was trotted out for Stubbs' benefit, Slate hadn't left his cage. It was as if Monzo and Pegg had forgotten him. The routine seemed unchanging with one subtle difference; two days after the last transformation, Pegg stopped visiting. As important an element as Pegg was in the situation, Slate expected him to be on hand all the time. His absence was a reassurance to Slate that for the moment, he would remain human. Slate was equally sure that Pegg would return with the full moon.

❖ ❖ ❖

The next afternoon, Slate heard two sets of footsteps. Monzo and Eddie stepped up to the cell. Slate took his usual stance, hands on the bars, elbows bent. It never hurts to be ready. Slate smiled and Monzo smiled in return. Neither spoke for minute then Eddie broke the tense silence. "You said you wanted to talk. So talk."

Slate ignored Eddie and looked straight at Monzo. "I think we got off to a bad start. I was pissed off at being abducted and caged with no idea what was going on. Now I have a pretty good handle on things. I think you've figured out by now what I am, that I'm for hire, and that I'm good at what I do. It seems a shame to let that all go to waste three weeks out of four. Assassination, demolition, spy stuff like wire taps; I could be a full time asset to you instead of just part time."

Monzo's poker face gave nothing away, but Slate was watching his eyes. Monzo's pupils dilated as Slate made his pitch, a "tell" that he was interested.

"I'm on the team whether I want to be or not, and in my, uh, situation, I have nowhere else to go. So, maybe I can be useful to you, in the off season, so to speak."

Monzo was silent for a full minute then said. "I'll think about it." Without another word, Monzo turned and walked away with Eddie trailing in his wake.

Slate listened to their retreating footsteps. The seed was planted. He picked up the dumbbells and did shoulder presses until his deltoids ached. Then he did curls.

❖ ❖ ❖

For the moment, the trouble between Stubbs and Monzo quieted down, but Monzo knew it wouldn't last. Whoever was behind the scenes invested too much time, effort, and money to give up after the first round. More would come, and when it did, there would be blood. Kovacks' hit on Monzo's men wasn't about the money. It was a plan to sow chaos in the organization. Tommy wasn't the target; the werewolf could have bitten any of the three, or God forbid, all of them. They were lucky with Tommy; Monzo hated to think what would have happened if three of his men changed at the same time, catching them totally unprepared.

And Vince, Monzo thought. I should have known it was too neat, too easy, when Vince popped up with the tip "from the street" that Kovacks took the money and killed Gino and his crew. Vince, the only one who didn't fire a shot at the werewolf in the bathtub, walked Tommy and Georgie right into the trap. Too bad Slate killed him before we could make him talk.

Monzo was counting on Vince's fear of the werewolf to loosen his tongue, but Vince wasn't afraid of Slate. He was afraid of something worse, and what that something worse might be gnawed at the back of Monzo's mind.

And now Slate. Logic told Monzo that Slate couldn't afford to turn on him, or to run. Without Pegg to control him, he'd go on a rampage that could end only in his death. His skills would be invaluable, but instinct told Monzo to leave Slate right where he was, and he did.

CHAPTER SEVENTEEN

As Slate expected, Pegg returned the first night of the full moon in August.

"So, Pegg, were you on vacation?"

Pegg smiled that odd v of his. "Nothing so mundane, Mr. Slate, nothing so mundane."

"I guess the full moon's on its way."

Pegg checked his watch. "In about ten minutes." He took the amulet from his pocket. "Let's make tonight easy." As promised. The moon rose right on time, and the transformation was almost gentle. The amulet's spell made a difference, but so did Slate's attitude. Instead of mind and body fighting the change, as Pegg had speculated, Slate was beginning to embrace it.

❖ ❖ ❖

That night Monzo took his pet for a walk.

Earlier that day Pegg was ushered into Monzo's office as soon as he came to the factory. "I want to take our boy to pay someone a visit tonight."

"And what do you want him to do on this visit?"

"I want him to persuade a fellow businessman that holding out on me is a bad idea."

John Acetone, "Johnny Ace" to his friends, owned a prosperous nightclub called The Cricket. Monzo wanted it. Johnny knew in the end he'd have to sell, but his greed outweighed his common sense. Monzo's offer was fair, full and up-front cash, but Johnny Ace wanted to bleed Monzo for all he could get. He told his friends, he resented "that Guinea prick Monzo" stepping in and taking over what he spent years building. He'd sell, but not until he made Monzo wait a while, just because he could.

Pegg pulled a small notebook from his coat. "Moonrise is at 10:38. We'll be ready to travel after 11:00."

❖ ❖ ❖

The Cricket was a quarter mile from what the Newark cops called The Battle Zone, the corridor of Prospect Boulevard that split the West End in half. The club's location kept its patrons safe from ghetto predators who knew better than to stray North of Prospect, but it lay close enough to the wild side to be a thrill for the civilians who packed the place night after night.

The front of the club was dark at 3:00 a.m., the bartenders, bouncers,

"Let's make tonight easy."

and waitresses gone for the night. The club that was so raucously noisy just a few hours before now lay eerily silent in the glow of the neon lights behind the bar.

Johnny Ace leaned back from the table in his chair with a glass of scotch looking at the tally for the past two weeks. Johnny was every inch the triple cliché of tall, dark and handsome, resplendent in a silk suit and a necktie that would cost some working stiff a week's wages. The Cricket was a success, a bigger success than he ever dreamed it would be. And that bastard Monzo was going to force him to sell. All the work, all the blood and sweat he put into the place and for what? To hand it over to that smug son of a bitch.

Monzo's words at their last meeting still stung him. "Johnny, nobody even has to know. I own it, you run it. For all anybody else knows, you're still the king." Monzo got one thing right, thought Johnny, in this place, I am the king, and my girl is the queen. Johnny looked across the table at Gloria. She looked terrific in that strapless emerald satin dress. Her blonde hair was a little mussed now, her lipstick a little blurry, but damn she looked like sex personified. How could he be a man for her if Monzo took his manhood away?

The phone jangled behind the bar. Carmen, Johnny's bodyguard answered it. "Johnny, it's for you. It's Paco. He says Monzo wants to see you at his place."

Johnny looked over at Gloria again and full of whisky bravado said to Carmen, "Tell him I'm busy. Tell him he wants to see me he can drag his sorry ass down here." He grinned and Gloria smiled back at him, her tongue showing between her teeth.

Carmen relayed the message and hung up the phone.

"What did he say?"

Carmen shrugged. "Nothin'. Just, 'Okay.'"

Outside across the street, Paco hung up the pay phone and stepped out of the booth. "He's in the club."

Inside, Johnny grinned and raised his drink to Gloria. "Here's to you, babe." He leaned forward over the table to kiss her.

At that moment, the glass doors of the club burst inward and a dark shape streaked across the dance floor, leapt over the bar and took Carmen off his feet. A scream and a gunshot then blood spattered in red fans across the mirrors. The Slate-wolf jumped onto the bar and crouched like a gargoyle, his maw dripping blood.

Gloria was too terrified to scream and Johnny Ace was too terrified to move.

"Sorry about the mess." Monzo strolled in flanked by Pegg and Eddie. Paco followed carrying a heavy duffel bag. "I'll have it cleaned up by tomorrow night. So, Johnny, now that I've dragged my sorry ass down here, what do you have to say for yourself?"

Johnny didn't look at Monzo. He was transfixed by the yellow eyes of the Slate-wolf blazing from the bar. Johnny's mouth opened and closed more than once, but no words came out.

Paco hefted the duffel bag onto the table and turned it over, dumping it out. It was filled with packets of money, twenties, fifties, and hundreds in bank wrappers. Johnny's eyes drifted to the mound of cash.

"It's all there, Johnny. Every dime I offered you for the place. I'm a man of my word, but you can count it if you want."

Paco reached into his suit and pulled out a sheaf of papers. He set them and a fountain pen on the table in front of Johnny. "It's an agreement of sale. Sign here and here."

Johnny hesitated, shaking his head, and Pegg said something in a whisper. Slate bounded from the bar, landing near Johnny's table. A low growl rumbled in Slate's chest and his mouth slowly peeled back to show his gore-clotted fangs.

Johnny picked up the pen in nerveless fingers and signed the papers.

Monzo smiled. "You know, Johnny, I was willing to let you stay on and run the place for me. It would have been our little secret, but I think now you'll be better off someplace else. I hear the Caymans are nice all year around." The smile disappeared as if someone threw a switch. "Don't show your face in this town again." Monzo turned to walk away and stopped. "Oh, there is one other small matter. About me being a guinea prick, let me show how big a prick I really am." He nodded to Pegg, who mouthed some words no one could hear but Slate.

The beast rose from its crouch, and strode to Gloria, its tongue slithering over its fangs.

"No! No!" Johnny shouted. He tried to rise from his chair, and Eddie and Paco pinned him to it. He tried to turn his head, avert his gaze, but Eddie grabbed a handful of Johnny's slick dark hair and forced him to face the unfolding scene.

The Slate-wolf delicately traced a dark finger from the hollow of Gloria's throat to the vee of her gown. A twitch of the paw, and the razor sharp claw slit the dress to her waist. Gloria's breasts spilled out of the split bodice. Her eyes bulged in terror as the beast licked her, tasting her, snuffling like a hound on a scent.

"No! No!"

"You had your chance, Johnny. You should have taken it."

The Slate-wolf lifted Gloria from the chair like a doll and threw her to the floor half under the table. Johnny couldn't see what was happening, but he could hear Gloria's shrieks and the rutting grunt of the beast. Tears ran down Johnny's cheeks. Long moments later Gloria's screams faded to a whimper, and the beast reared its head in a howl of obscene triumph.

"Good night, Johnny," said Monzo. "It's been a pleasure doing business with you."

CHAPTER EIGHTEEN

The next day, Brae got a message from Monzo telling him to come that night at ten thirty. Brae was accustomed to Monzo's demands and his spur-of-the-moment summonses. His sources told him that Monzo now owned The Cricket and that Johnny Acetone left town with no forwarding address. Brae knew the deal was in the works and that Johnny Ace was balking. Maybe tonight he'd find out exactly how it all came down.

The meeting would also give Brae a chance to learn what was going on with Monzo and the werewolf. Monzo never mentioned Tommy or werewolves or a man named Pegg. Maybe tonight he would take Brae into his confidence. Brae pulled his Mercedes to the gate outside the factory and blew three short blasts on his horn. In a moment the gate rolled back with a jangling and a clank of a chain and sprocket. As he drove toward the factory entrance, the gate closed behind him.

At the entrance to the building, Brae met two guards, hitters from Monzo's inner circle. One opened the door as the other kept his eyes on the parking lot and his hands on what Brae recognized as an M-16 automatic rifle. It could shoot 30 rounds through a steel helmet or a bulletproof vest on full auto. Only the military was supposed to have them, but somehow a few found their way into Monzo's hands.

Paco led Brae into Monzo's office. Eddie sat in one chair, and a tall, strange looking man sat in another. Monzo waited until Paco quietly closed the door before speaking. "Carson, thank you for coming."

"You know I'm here for you always, Michael," Brae said, taking a third chair.

"This is Mr. Pegg."

Brae turned to face Pegg, who took off his dark glasses. Brae felt himself being weighed, sifted and plumbed by a presence as potent as The

Whisperer, but it almost felt like fingertips brushing over his skin without penetrating to the soul inside. What was it The Whisperer said? Shielded? Brae nodded, maintaining his composure; years in the courtroom taught him well. "Pleased to meet you." Brae was grateful that Pegg sat too far away for a handshake.

Pegg's face folded into its amused smile. "And I am pleased to meet you as well, Mr. Brae. Mr. Monzo speaks highly about you."

"I'm afraid I can't say the same about you. In fact Mr. Monzo has never mentioned you at all." He turned his gaze to Monzo. "Have you, Michael?"

"No, Carson, up to now, the two of you have operated in, shall we say, separate compartments, but some things have come up, and I think you need to know about them. Last night, I concluded my deal with Johnny Ace to buy The Cricket. The circumstance was, shall we say, less than amicable, but I now own the club. I need you to file the appropriate papers, expedite the liquor and cabaret licenses, and generally grease the wheels for the, uh, transition."

Monzo handed a sheaf of papers to Brae. Brae recognized them as the sale agreement he drew up weeks before when Monzo began his negotiations for the nightclub. A small red splash marked the signature page. "Michael, is this Johnny's blood?"

Monzo shook his head slowly. "No."

"I won't ask whose. Michael, if you got him to sign this agreement under duress, it could invalidate the whole thing. What if he takes it to court?"

"He won't be around to do that." Monzo smiled and Eddie chuckled.

"You didn't kill him."

Monzo rolled his cigar between his thumb and index finger. "Johnny and his sweetheart are very much alive, even as we speak, but we won't hear from him again. We used a form of persuasion that he couldn't refuse." Monzo stood up. "Mr. Pegg, is it time?"

Pegg looked at his watch. "Eight minutes."

"Come on, Carson, let's take a walk. There's somebody I want you to meet."

In his cell, Slate waited for moonrise. It would arrive soon, and Pegg hadn't shown up yet. Slate dreaded the transformation without Pegg's assistance, but he would tough it out. Number one priority: survive.

He heard several pairs of footsteps approach, and in a moment, Monzo, Eddie, and Pegg stood before him along with a tall, distinguished man in a grey suit.

"Carson." Said Monzo, "This is Mr. Slate. Mr. Slate, this is my attorney Carson Brae."

Brae's brow creased in puzzlement. Slate's face was impassive as he took Brae's measure. Throw him in with me, thought Slate. He's got some reach on me and he's in good shape, but I don't need the beast to take him down.

Brae turned to Monzo. "Michael, I don't understand."

"You will in a moment. Mr. Pegg?"

"Thirty seconds."

❖ ❖ ❖

Moonrise.

The change came over Slate, and this time, Pegg didn't offer his help. Slate raged and snarled and threw himself at the bars, clawing between them at Brae. "My God." As Brae watched, despite his knowledge and his terror at what the Whisperer had done to him, his startled fear was no less genuine as he watched Slate become a monster.

"Now, counselor, a legal question: You've met Slate and you've seen what he becomes. If this thing kills someone, is John Slate the human guilty of murder?"

CHAPTER NINETEEN

The next night was uneventful. The change came and went, and Slate didn't leave his cell. The fourth night Pegg came as usual but brought his chair with him.

Slate looked through the high window of his cell at the fading sky. "So, what's on the card for tonight? Who do I scare this time?"

"No one. Tonight will be a quiet evening at home, as it were. I'm here to see to that." When the moon rose, the change was painless, and Pegg's voice told the Slate-wolf, "Peace. Rest." And Slate obeyed. In a moment, he was asleep.

❖ ❖ ❖

While Pegg visited Slate, outside, a dark Cadillac parked in the shadow of a warehouse a quarter mile from Monzo's headquarters. In it, two men waited. The driver said, in his Irish accent, "And would this be close enough for you, Mr. Kovacks?"

The burly blond passenger did not reply. He understood little English and spoke less. Since Mr. Smith spoke no Romanian, their communication was nil, but Smith was amused by the pretense. "Then if you would be so kind as to step out." Smith reached across Kovacks and opened the passenger door. "Himself likes me to keep his car clean you know." He chuckled at the thought that he could have told Kovacks to go to the Devil, or that his mother was a baboon, or nearly anything, so long as he kept a straight face. He made a shooing gesture and Kovacks stepped out of the car and into the alley.

Kovacks left the car and stood impassive, arms folded, watching the sky. Brae explained the layout of Monzo's headquarters to the Whisperer earlier that day, and the Whisperer told Kovacks where to find the Enemy.

Mr. Smith reached into the pocket of his shabby brown suit and pulled out an amulet identical to Pegg's. Kovacks exercised marvelous self control but it never hurt to play it safe.

Moonrise.

Monzo had posted guards in pairs outside the factory since the trouble began. Tonight it was Frankie and Mario at the front of the building and Mick and Georgie at the rear. Their job was simple: shoot anyone who came near, no questions asked.

Georgie stood in the doorway, a *lupo*, a short sawed-off shotgun cradled in his hands. Georgie's eyes darted nervously back and forth. Mick was more laid back. He was in the middle of lighting a cigarette when a dark blur shot noiselessly over the chain link fence and the barbed wire at the back of the lot. The glare of the match in his eyes kept him from seeing it, but Georgie caught it in the edge of his vision. He brought up his shotgun and started to shout a warning to Mick but before he could pull the triggers, a blow from a fist like a furred hammer pounded his face in as if it were a cardboard mask.

The beast was cunning. It took Georgie first because Mick's hands were occupied with his cigarette. He pulled his automatic as the diabolical golden eyes turned on him. Mick got off two shots before a paw sliced through his stomach like a scoop through a dish of sorbet and hurled a thick gob of his entrails against the side of the building with a sickening splatter. Mick fell onto his back and his last thought was that the cigarette that fell from his slack lips was burning his cheek.

The Kovacks-beast howled at the kill but didn't stop to savor its reward. It hurled itself against the steel door once, twice, and on the third strike took it from its hinges. The crash echoed through the building, and the beast that was Laszlo Kovacks sped to the stairs that led to Monzo's office.

Below, Pegg heard the gunfire, the crash and the howl. Behind him in the darkness, the Tommy-wolf howled at the invader's presence. Pegg gripped the silver medallion and his mind raced. He made a decision and unlocked the door of Slate's cell. "Intruder," Pegg said. "Hunt. Kill."

The words yanked Slate back from his peaceful repose and in a second, he exploded through the open door, a howling mass of fury. Pegg started after him, but an impulse made him turn and head for Tommy's cell.

Monzo's office door was as secure as a bank vault, but that didn't stop Kovacks from trying to batter his way inside. When the door didn't yield, Kovacks began hurling himself against the wall. It began to buckle inward, and it was only a matter of minutes before Kovacks would gorge himself on Monzo's flesh.

Three of Monzo's gunmen lay in bloody tatters in the outer office, and a fourth sprawled on the stairs. Slate leapt over him and burst into the outer office, stoked by the scent of fresh blood and death. He wanted desperately to thrust his snout into the blood and gore, but Pegg's command filled him with single minded purpose: kill the intruder.

Kovacks sensed Slate's presence and whirled to meet his attacker. The pair hurled themselves at each other scattering chairs and desks and collided with bone-crunching impact. The werewolves grappled furiously, rolling over and over on the blood slick floor, jaws snapping and eyes blazing with hatred.

Instinct took over. Slate put a clawed foot into Kovacks' abdomen and flipped him head over heels to crash into a row of filing cabinets. Before Slate could get to his feet, Kovacks was on him again, slashing at him viciously with his claws. Slate sunk his fangs into Kovacks' forearm, but the werewolf clubbed Slate's head away. Locked in a death-struggle, the pair rolled over desks and smashed chairs and tables. Kovacks swung a paw at Slate, catching him on the side of his head and ripping his face open in three parallel gashes.

Slate responded with a swipe that barely missed Kovacks' throat. As good a fighter as Slate was, Kovacks was simply better, more practiced at being a monster. And then, Slate slipped on the bloody floor and fell to his back. Kovacks leapt upon him, struggling to get his slavering jaws within striking distance of Slate's throat. Slate kept Kovacks at bay, but a dim corner of his mind told him that soon Kovacks would wear him down and kill him.

His inner voice urged: Survive.

From the doorway, a furred horror threw itself with a howl onto Kovacks, pulling him from Slate. Tommy slashed at Kovacks, snarling in fury. In the doorway, Pegg held the amulet high and focused his attention on Kovacks, but his power wasn't strong enough to control all three werewolves at once. The fight was quick and vicious. Tommy fought hard, but Kovacks closed on him and delivered a disemboweling slash followed by a snap of his jaws on Tommy's throat. Kovacks tipped his head back and howled in victory.

His howl was cut short as Slate drove into him, knocking them both through the window in an explosion of glass. They fell to the ground two stories below with an impact that would have shattered human bones and they bounced apart. Both rose, warily circling each other in the faint silver moonglow. Over Kovacks' shoulder, Slate saw that the moon was no longer round, but an ebbing crescent. Kovacks roared and charged, but Slate deftly dodged his rush. One more minute and...

Eclipse.

Slate and Kovacks felt the change begin at the same instant. Both felt it end, and with it the reins of control. The pair faced each other in the dark, bloody, battered, and absolutely human. Slate's teeth bared in a wicked grin as Kovacks rushed him. Kovacks was more practiced at fighting as a wolf, but Slate was more practiced at fighting as a man.

Slate slipped to the side and swept Kovacks' feet from under him. Kovacks fell, rolling with the momentum of his charge. Before he stopped, Slate dove onto him, driving a knee into his kidneys and a forearm into the base of his skull. Kovacks was desperate and he was strong. He rolled over, throwing Slate off, but in an instant, Slate was at him again with a flurry of punishing kicks and punches. Slate cross kicked Kovacks' knee, shattering the bones, and Kovacks fell. Slate leapt onto his back, and with a sharp two-handed twist, broke Kovacks' neck leaving his dead face staring over his shoulder.

Survive.

Escape.

Slate rose to his feet and walked toward the door where Frankie and Mario stood openmouthed, realizing too late the threat Slate posed. Slate grinned. "Hey guys." Frankie raised his pistol but Slate caught the gun hand and spun Frankie in front of him as a shield before Mario could get off a shot. He put his finger over Frankie's and pulled the trigger.

The back of Mario's head sprayed the wall behind him. Slate yanked Frankie's arm upward, putting the muzzle of the automatic under his chin and blew off the top of his head.

Monzo and Pegg clattered down the stairs, Eddie close behind jacking a shell filled with silver buckshot into a riot gun. By the time they got outside, Slate was over the fence and swallowed by the darkness.

Monzo lost all his composure. He shouted at Pegg. "Stop him! Call him back!" He grabbed Pegg by the lapels of his coat and screamed in his face. "Do something!"

Even in the darkness, Pegg's eyes found Monzo's. Monzo released his grip on the wizard's coat and he stumbled backward. "The eclipse broke the spell. He has to be in my presence for me to invoke it again."

"You knew about the eclipse," Monzo snarled. "You knew this would happen."

"I wanted to see how the eclipse would affect Slate, but of course I expected him to be in the cell the whole time. I wouldn't have let him out had I not thought it were necessary. Perhaps you would rather I just let him," he pointed to Kovacks' twisted body, "visit your office."

Eddie piped up, "But we coulda shot his ass when he turned human."

Pegg looked over the top of his glasses at Eddie. "If he turned human soon enough, you could have. I did not know how quickly they would turn, and my guess is that this one would have been through the wall in plenty of time to twist your thick head off that thick neck of yours. I made a judgment call. It was a calculated risk."

"And now Slate's gone," said Monzo, and Tommy's dead. You've got to find him, Pegg."

Pegg looked up at the waxing moon. "I think the trail he leaves may be simple enough to follow. Besides, if I read Mr. Slate correctly, he will be back."

In the distance, a long howl echoed through the moonlit night. Monzo's eyes stared wide into the distant shadows. Eddie's hair rose on the back of his neck. The howl sounded again.

Escape.

Payback.

❖ ❖ ❖

Mr. Smith drove slowly back to the town house, in no rush to bear bad news. Himself will not be pleased, he thought. The eclipse was an oversight. Up to now, Kovacks was responsible for himself and all of the attendant details of his transformation; no intermediary was necessary, and the Master's obsessive secretiveness led him to smuggle the Romanian into the country and to isolate him as he did the team that robbed the La-Ja. The Master kept the lycanthrope ignorant of English, leaving Kovacks able to speak only with him. If Kovacks knew the perils of an eclipse, apparently his inability to understand English prevented him from hearing or reading about it. Or perhaps one had never occurred since he was turned, as infrequent as they were. In any case, Mr. Smith braced himself for the anger that he knew was waiting at the town house. He was not the object of that anger, but that fact made it no less unpleasant.

CHAPTER TWENTY

Slate's night was spent in wild exhilaration. He was out of his cage and running free, the moon shining on his monstrous face, and his imprisonment lay behind him. The cool night air filled his lungs, and the dew-wet grass delighted his feet after the concrete floor of his cage. He ran, and he ran, and he ran, leaping fences, darting from shadow to black shadow, staying out of sight. The most basic of responses: fight or flee; Slate had done both.

Something was different in his condition. The eclipse and the rapid transformation back and forth somehow weakened the barrier between the human and the beast. The savage side of him wanted to stay at the factory and tear every one of his tormentors limb from limb, but his human half told him that the controller was there and would put him back into the cage if he didn't flee. Reason was returning. So he ran.

The Slate-wolf found cover in a copse of trees along the fairway of a golf course. He felt pain from the slashes in his face and from the blows of the monster he killed. When the transformation came at moonset, the agony was severe but a fair price for his freedom.

When the moon set, the sky was still dark and Slate's time sense told him it would stay dark for at least two more hours. He took inventory. His canvas shirt and trousers were ripped and spattered with blood. He looked like the escaped prisoner he was. He was barefoot, broke and unarmed in hostile territory. He smiled. Business as usual.

CHAPTER TWENTY-ONE

Daybreak found Slate dressed in jeans and a work shirt, steel-toed boots on his feet. The Sears Roebuck department store in a nearby shopping center was an easy break-in after he put a sleeper hold on the watchman and took his keys. Slate could have easily killed him, but decided against it. The cops would look a lot harder for a murderer than they would for a burglar. Instead, he bound the watchman hand and foot, gagged him, and left him in a store room.

The Sears Roebuck store was a treasure trove for Slate. After he dressed, he stuffed a change of clothes in a duffel bag and headed for the sporting goods department. He chose a lightweight sleeping bag and stuffed it into a second duffel along with an armload of dehydrated food packs, a water purifying kit and a plastic tarp. A display of knives yielded an eight-inch Case hunting knife and a classic Swiss Army pocketknife with multiple tool blades. A camp hatchet and sharpening stone rounded out the tools. The selection of guns was small, but Slate found a Mossberg 12-gauge pump whose action was smooth. Five minutes in the hardware department, and with the help of a Sears' Best Craftsman hacksaw, the Mossberg was cut down to fit in the duffel along with two boxes of shells, one box of double-aught buckshot, one of deer slugs.

The watchman's wallet had a little cash, a driver's license with the name Edward Collins, and the registration card for the 1964 Ford Falcon parked in the loading dock. Not the greatest ride for a getaway car, and Slate knew that when someone noticed it was missing, the cops would put out an APB, so he'd dump it in an hour or two anyway. One last item; Slate checked the break room refrigerator and found the watchman's lunch in a paper sack.

Food, clothing, shelter, money, weapons. There was nothing like Sears Roebuck in Laos, Slate thought as he pulled the Falcon away from the loading dock. Another satisfied customer.

Survive.

Escape.

Slate headed west to throw off pursuers, the rising sun at his back. In an hour, he'd leave the Falcon, steal another car, maybe a pickup truck or a Jeep with four-wheel drive and head for the Garden State Parkway, a straight line to the world's greatest hideout. The Pine Barrens were waiting; more than a million acres of desolate, overgrown pine forest sprawling over seven New Jersey counties. A hundred yards from the highway and a man would be swallowed up by the forest. Finding Slate there would be a chore for even the most experienced investigators and trackers. Trained as he was in survival skills, with a plastic tarp, a coffee can and a hunting knife, Slate could hide and elude detection, let alone capture indefinitely.

And the deep woods would allow him a safe space to transform without harming anyone or being seen. It would give him time to think his way out of his predicament and to consider revenge. In the meantime he needed somebody to watch his back and to restrain him when he changed. It was a tough call, but he decided to break his silence and try to contact the team.

❖ ❖ ❖

In Newark, Monzo poured himself another scotch and pondered his situation. Slate was gone. His werewolf was gone, and with Tommy dead, Pegg couldn't make another easily, if at all. Monzo didn't know magic, but he did know people. So far, only Pegg and a few of his men knew that Slate was gone, and as long as people like Stubbs thought he was still on hand, Monzo kept his advantage. The word was whispered around town that Monzo had a new enforcer, one that bullets couldn't stop and that killed without mercy. The rumors flew and the rumors grew and Monzo did nothing to discourage them.

Meanwhile, Monzo had a new project, The Cricket. The club reopened without a hitch after a day off to fix the doors and mop up the blood, and the crowd seemed bigger than ever. A few people asked about Johnny Ace, but in a week he'd be forgotten. In the meantime, the money laundering operation at The Cricket went on as usual but without Johnny Ace's cut. Like Monzo told Brae, *mezza mezza.*

Pegg had saved them all by letting both the werewolves loose, but in solving one problem, Pegg opened a box full of new ones. Things were quiet for the moment, but they couldn't stay that way for long. Monzo had to find Slate. He put the word out all over Jersey, New York and Pennsylvania, and Pegg had his feelers out too. So far, nothing turned up, and the trail got colder every day. Something Pegg said nagged at the back of Monzo's mind: "If I read Mr. Slate correctly, he will be back." Monzo was certain he would. If I read him correctly, thought Monzo, he's not the kind to let things lie.

The Whisperer sat unmoving. He'd not moved for almost an hour by Mr. Smith's calculation, but that was not unusual. Mr. Smith simply sat still as well and waited. Himself would speak when he was ready. The Whisperer had underestimated Monzo and didn't expect him to have the resources to handle the werewolf or to kill Kovacks. The man seemed to have the Devil in his pocket. But according to Mr. Smith, one of Monzo's werewolves died in the fight and the other escaped. Mr. Smith had the medallion, half the battle. He need only find the surviving werewolf, a fellow named Slate, and things would resume as they were. The field was level between Monzo and Stubbs once again.

Wheels within wheels within wheels; to achieve his larger ends the Whisperer needed power and money was the short path to power in this world. The drug trade seemed to be the quickest way to both but proved to be more difficult to broach than he expected. Perhaps it was time to talk with Mr. Stubbs.

CHAPTER TWENTY-TWO

Slate lay on his stomach under a tree. Leaves and twigs covered all of him but his eyes. He had been waiting for two hours and finally the herd of deer he'd been stalking for two days came to drink in the pool a few yards away. A buck, two does and three dappled fawns. The buck was a spike, his antlers likely in the hardening stage by now. He kept his head up watching, wary, as the others drank from the green-edged pond. Because the cut-down shotgun was less accurate than most deer rifles, Slate opted to wait to shoot until the deer were in a cluster and he was more likely to hit one.

The buck lowered his head to the pool. He stood between Slate and one of the does. This was probably the best shot he'd have. Slate sighted down the short barrel and squeezed the trigger. The gun roared and all the deer scattered but one. The buck fell halfway into the water. Slate climbed from his blind and headed over to gut the kill.

Dressing the deer was quick work, and the reward was welcome. He'd been living for days on the camping meals and fresh venison would be a good source of protein. He cut away the backstraps and tenderloins and washed the blood from them in the pool. He then dragged the carcass back to his blind and covered it with leaves and brush. There were enough scavenger animals in the Barrens to take care of the remains. Slate regretted wasting good meat but he had no time or means to cure it and moving every day as he did, carrying it would be inconvenient.

Squirrels and rabbits were plentiful but Slate wanted to use the shotgun sparingly. Besides conserving ammunition, he wasn't sure about hunting regulations and didn't want to attract attention from some overzealous game warden. The area Slate chose was so desolate that he had seen only a handful of people since he entered the Pine Barrens, most of them hunters, and none of them had seen him. One stood out, a heavy set man who carried a camera and a shoulder bag and wore a green Guinness cap with a long bill. A nature photographer, thought Slate. Plenty to shoot out here with a camera or a gun, and the man in the green cap carried both. What looked like a .357 magnum hung in a holster on his hip.

One other sign of civilization was a good sized marijuana patch, obviously tended with great care. Slate spotted it from a distance and skirted it carefully. He watched the ground along the trail looking for snares and trip wires, and near the patch, he saw a gleam of metal. It had rained the night before and some of the soil was washed away from the

Slate…headed over to gut the kill.

shiny hack-sawed edge of a piece of tubing. He carefully scraped away more of the dirt with his knife and exposed a nasty booby trap.

The tubing was pushed four inches into the earth and a shotgun shell was wedged snugly in the bottom. Below it, the tube was arranged to push the primer onto the point of a nail, firing the shell through the foot of anyone unlucky enough to step on it hard enough. Slate saw the same kind of trap or variations of it all over Viet Nam; cheap, easily deployed, and disabling, if not fatal. Whoever tended this weed patch had been over and met Charlie. Also, he was a sociopath who didn't give a damn who he hurt; either that or a sadist who got off on the idea.

Slate carefully dug the trap out of the ground and threw it into the woods. He replaced the soil and threw some leaves and duff over the spot. Then he carefully struck out through the dense brush at a right angle to the trail away from the hazard zone. He knew there were other people around. Now he knew just how dangerous they were. There goes the neighborhood.

A few days before he shot the deer, Slate had spent a half day hitchhiking to Camden and found a public library with in the periodical section. There he sat at a table to read the personal ads carefully looking for any of the contact codes his team used. Nothing today or the three previous days the library had on hand. The library had typewriters available for use, and after bumming a sheet of paper and an envelope from the librarian he typed an ad of his own for the *Times*: Rainy day. Need a tent. He wrapped the paper around the money to pay for the ad and sealed the envelope. A six cent stamp from a vending machine and the ad was on its way to New York.

Slate stayed overnight in Camden in a cheap transient hotel and the next day returned to the library. He spent hours looking for information about werewolves. He didn't find much, most of it encyclopedia entries, and the few things he found were often contradictory from source to source. Smith writes that werewolves can't cross running water and Jones writes that they can. Jones writes that werewolves are repelled by wolfbane and marigolds and Smith writes that only wolfbane works as a protection. He also learned that much of the common lore of the werewolf came not from folk tales but from the imaginations of Hollywood scriptwriters inventing fantastic circumstances when reality was incredible enough. Slate concluded that if he wanted information he would have to get it from someone who knew what werewolves were really about. He would have to get it from Pegg, which meant returning to Newark, but in the meantime he would have to face a full moon alone.

❖ ❖ ❖

In Nags Head, North Carolina head librarian Marie Saville shook her head disapprovingly at the scruffy transient who sat in one of the library's overstuffed chairs reading A few months ago he'd just shown up and once or twice a week would sit down with the week's newspapers and read through them. If he liked New York so much, she wished he'd go there instead of loafing in her library. At least he didn't smell as bad as some of the derelicts who came in out of the rain to loiter.

Mike Haines leaned back in the comfortable chair, grateful for the library's air conditioning in the mid-day heat. He ran his fingers over the blonde stubble on his chin. Shaving wasn't a priority but he reminded himself that people judged you first by your looks. The rolled sleeves of his chambray work shirt showed arms that testified to strength without bulk. His forearms were long and lean, tendons pushing at the skin beside corded muscle, ending in broad scarred hands. He picked up the first of the group of newspapers he took from the rack; four days of the *New York Times* to check. So far, no word from the team; for all Mike knew, they could all be lounging on beaches in Maui or Bora-Bora, but he doubted that.

They were sold out by a gang of politicians and bureaucrats and some good people were killed because of it. People would pay, in time. But first he had to find his friends. Wednesday's paper had the ad: Rainy day. Need a tent. Haines copied the ad and jotted down the classified address on a scrap of paper. He didn't know which of the team placed the ad but it was in their code. Rainy day: trouble; need a tent: need help. Later that day Haines mailed an ad of his own: Rainy day, have tent will travel; count the days.

CHAPTER TWENTY-THREE
MOONRISE.

The first unaided change went more easily than Slate thought it might. Maybe he was becoming accustomed to it. Maybe a part of him was welcoming the power the change represented, a thought he tried to keep at bay. He spent the day pushing as deep into the woods as he could go and as far away from possible human encounters as he could be when the moon rose over the pines. Slate stripped to a pair of cut off jeans and concealed his clothes along with his gear and sat cross-legged on a bed of pine needles waiting for the tingling to begin.

To change in freedom was exhilarating. The freedom from Pegg's control was even more so. The forest was home, unlike the cage in Monzo's headquarters. He howled exultantly and ran through the silvery night like the wild creature he was. The moon set shortly before sunrise, and Slate returned to humanity remembering more about his time as a werewolf than he did before. There was blood on him, but with its scent came the memory of a deer he chased through the darkness, leaping on its back, sinking his fangs into its neck; the spurting blood steaming in the chill of night and the rich taste of quivering flesh. Slate walked for some time before he reached his clothing; he'd gone farther than he expected and was forced to search for landmarks.

Another issue was his feet. Slate's bare soles were calloused and tough, but roots, thistles, and stones in the sandy soil ignored by the running beast made the long walk on human feet painful. Slate washed away the dried blood and spread his bedroll in the concealment of heavy brush. Time to rest, to sleep; the night would come too soon.

CHAPTER TWENTY-FOUR

A twig snapped. Slate jackknifed awake, grabbing the shotgun and thumbing off the safety. In the clearing twenty yards away a man was carefully picking his way toward Slate's concealment. He was in his twenties, small, skinny, and dressed in a dun canvas jacket over jeans and green rubber boots. Long, stringy hair hung from a greasy red leather baseball-cap. He carried a bolt-action rifle at the ready, finger on the trigger. He peered at the ground, stepping carefully around twigs and dry leaves.

He stopped and his head turned toward Slate's patch of brush. He took a step toward it and an arm whipped around his neck, cutting off his wind and the point of a knife appeared at the corner of his eye. "Open the bolt and drop the rifle." Slate spoke softly in his ear; his voice was cold, chilling in fact. When the redneck hesitated, Slate pushed the point of the knife into his eyelid at the top of the socket. "Now."

The bolt clattered and a gleaming shell sprung from the rifle. The rifle fell to the ground. "Hands in front of you. Fingers. How many more of you?" The captive put up one finger. Slate took the knife away from the redneck's eye. He sagged in relief in Slate's grip, and then Slate drove the pommel of the knife into his temple. Slate lowered him to the ground without a sound. Fifty yards away a voice called, "Jim? Where the hell are you?" Time to run. Slate circled the clearing to pick up his gear. He was just reaching for the shotgun when a voice to his right too close to be real said, "Stay still, Bud. A rifle cracked and the shotgun spun out of reach. "Next one goes in your knee."

There was a sharp whistle and a response. Then a mass of leaves moved and stood up like a living haystack; a man in a sniper's ghillie suit. The barrel of a rifle pointed through the camouflage at Slate's head. "Took us three days to find you. I admit you were good, but I'm just a little bit better."

Another man in hunting clothes entered the clearing behind Slate. "Danny, the sumbitch killed Jim!"

Danny, the ghillie man, said, "Not likely, Cameron. He's just knocked out. Get over here and keep your weapon on this one." Slate heard rustling behind him and felt the muzzle of a gun between his shoulder blades.

"Back up, you damned fool. He'll spin and have your weapon up your ass before you can pull the trigger. Don't you remember anything I taught you?" Cameron backed away, and Danny pulled back the ghillie suit hood. Danny's face was a weathered tan, his forehead split by a thin white scar from his hairline across the bridge of his nose to the top of his right cheek. His eyes were a feral green and his blond hair was cut in a boot camp buzz.

"We knew there was somebody out here but it took a while to pin you down." He pointed his rifle at Slate's torso. Over Slate's shoulder he told Cameron, "Tie his hands and hobble his feet. We got some walking to do." He looked back to Slate, "And then you got some talking to do."

Slate's hands were tied behind his back and rope was knotted at both ankles with about two feet between allowing him to walk but not run. Cameron and Danny slapped Jim awake and pulled him to his feet, and the four of them started through the woods. No blindfold, thought Slate. They don't care who I see or what I see. Before they left the site, they packed his gear and left no trace he was ever there. They plan to kill me, he thought, but what comes first?

The walk took nearly an hour by Slate's time sense, and his captors hardly spoke. The trek ended in a clearing at a ramshackle cabin made of rough-sawn boards. Old car parts and other nondescript junk littered the yard. To one side of the cabin Slate saw an A-frame with a chain hoist. The area around it was cluttered with bones and antlers.

Danny turned to Slate and looked over his shoulder. He nodded to Jim and Jim slammed the butt of his rifle into the base of Slate's skull. Slate fell forward like a sack of sand.

❖ ❖ ❖

When he woke, Slate found himself tied to an old wooden chair in the yard in front of the cabin, his ankles lashed tightly to its legs. A length of greasy rope wound around his chest and the chair back a half dozen times and was firmly knotted behind him. Slate wasn't going anywhere. Jim leered at him. "Think you're so goddamn tough. He spat in Slate's face then as an afterthought hit him with a roundhouse that loosened two of Slate's molars. In a few minutes, Slate's left eye was swollen shut, both his lips were split and his nose was probably broken.

Danny walked out of the cabin. "That'll do, Jim. I think you softened him up enough." Danny's ghilie suit hung from a nearby tree and he now wore a denim jacket over grease-stained jeans and a ratty T-shirt. He squatted in the dirt in front of Slate. We found a driver's license in your stuff, but I know damned well your name isn't Edward Collins. So tell me, what is it?

Slate looked him squarely in the eye and said nothing.

"I think you're stubborn. I think you've been taught to be, but so have I." Danny pulled a Ka-Bar hunting knife from his boot and drew it gently across Slate's thigh. Slate felt the pinch, and in a few seconds, blood soaked into the fabric of his jeans. "Keep it simple. Tell me who you're working for."

Slate didn't flinch and didn't speak. Over Danny's shoulder, he saw the last edge of the sun dipping below the treetops. Keep them talking.

"You sure as hell aren't a tourist on a camping trip. Who hired you to spy on us?"

"Spy?" Slate laughed.

"I say you're a narc."

A light went on in Slate's head. "That's your weed patch? And those are your traps? When were you over?"

Danny ignored the question. "So you found the weed and the traps. And I'll bet you're the sumbitch who dug up one or two and threw them away."

"I can't believe you clowns. Anybody could have set off those traps; a hunter, a Boy Scout troop on a nature hike..."

"Or maybe your buddy that cameraman, huh?" Jim broke in. "He working with you?" Danny turned to Jim and said sharply, "Shut up, Jim. One thing at a time. Are you a narc?"

"Does it matter? You're going to kill me anyway, right?"

"I'll ask you one more time: are you a narc?"

Slate shook his head. Keep them talking. "Hell no."

"Okay, then, who you working for? You scouting us for somebody else's operation?"

Slate decided a little bit of truth could go a long way. "I came here because it's a good place to hide."

Jim jumped in. "Hide? From who? You bringing the cops in here after you?"

"No, no cops." Slate smiled to the side of his split lips. "I guess you could say the other team is looking for me."

Danny's expression changed from arrogance to calculation. "You mean gangsters? The Mafia?" The three of them traded glances. "That changes everything," said Danny. "Our friend here may be worth a lot to us."

Cameron looked puzzled. "How?"

Danny smiled and said, not to Cameron but to Slate. "I was Special Forces in 'Nam; did two tours, and while I was over there, I watched and I learned. I saw how much money there was to be made selling weed, so when I come back here, I started growing my own. People around here might buy a nickel or a dime's worth, but they don't buy by the ton. My brothers and I need a connection, somebody who'll buy our grass in bulk. You tell us who's after you, and we hand you over, maybe the big boys'll do business with us."

"You think the Mob will bother with a bunch of half-wit hillbillies like you three?" Slate grinned although it hurt his lips. "Don't make me laugh."

Jim swung his fist at Slate's head, but Danny caught his wrist. "Don't waste your time hitting him. It hasn't worked up to now and it won't." He stood up and stepped away from Slate's chair, motioning the others to follow. They stood, heads together talking quietly and reached a decision.

The three picked Slate up, chair and all, and set him in front of the A-frame. Cameron kicked the chair over face first into the packed dirt. Slate heard the ratcheting of the block and tackle, heard the chain clink as they threaded it through the ropes between his feet and felt the tug as the block and tackle yanked him off the ground. Jim laughed and spun the chair. The deepening shadows whirled across Slate's line of vision. Where was the moon?

Danny came out of the cabin screwing the brass works of a propane torch onto a blue cylinder. Cameron pulled their pickup truck into the clearing so that the headlights shone on the A-frame. Danny caught Slate by the leg and stopped his spinning. He turned the dial on the regulator and propane hissed out of the torch. Danny scratched a match with his thumbnail, and in a second, a blue tongue of flame shot from the torch's nozzle. He looked down at Slate's face. "I guess you know what happens next. Gonna tell me who's looking for you?"

Slate closed his eyes. Survive. Escape. Payback.

Slate didn't answer, and Danny set the torch on the ground, the flame inches from Slate's eyes. He grabbed the edges of the cut in Slate's jeans and ripped the denim away, baring Slate's thigh. He squinted at glossy patches of scar tissue where skin had been flayed in square inches. "Well, well, well."

"What is it?" said Jim.

"Seems our friend here is no virgin. This may take a while."

Danny dialed the torch's flame down to a fine blue point. "Last call, Bud."

He touched the tip of the flame lightly to Slate's leg and in spite of himself, Slate jerked in the chair and didn't scream but instead snarled in pain. Danny looked at the blistering flesh, almost a perfect circle from the torch's tip. He burned a second spot beside it. Slate gritted his teeth and held back a scream.

Danny shook a Lucky from the pack in his t-shirt pocket and put it in his mouth. He lit it from the end of the torch. He burned a third patch on Slate's thigh, a little larger, a little deeper. Cameron gagged at the smell of charred flesh, but Jim and Danny were unaffected. Slate bucked against the ropes and roared through his clenched teeth.

Cameron said, "How come he ain't talking?"

Danny said, "Cause he's one hard-assed sumbitch. Take off his boots and lower him a little."

The chain rattled and Slate's head and shoulders hit the ground. Cameron started to cut away the laces of the first boot when Jim slapped his hand away. "No, you goddamn idiot; them's good boots. Don't ruin 'em." In a moment, Slate could see his bare feet in the headlights.

Danny held the torch a few inches from Slate's toes. "You know, our mama used to play a game with us when we was little. This little piggy went to market." Danny brought the tip of the flame to Slate's little toe and held it steady as it burned him to the bone. The flesh sizzled in the intense heat. "This little piggy stayed home." Danny stepped back and took a drag from his Lucky. Cameron turned away and retched. Jim's eyes gleamed. "This little piggy had roast beef." This time Slate screamed. "This little piggy had…what the hell?" Danny stared openmouthed as Slate's foot bulged and swelled, bones popping, claws erupting from his charred toes.

Moonrise.

The change was violent. The chair snapped into kindling as Slate thrashed in its throes. The brothers jumped back and stared in amazement. In seconds, the Slate-wolf burst its bonds and came howling at them. Jim was the closest. Slate drove his claws through Jim's gut all the way to his vertebrae. Blood spurted from Jim's mouth as Slate's paw wrapped around Jim's spine. One swipe of the other paw ripped away his agonized face like a Halloween mask, leaving a more horrible one in its place. The howling Slate pounded Jim against the trunk of a nearby tree pulverizing bones and spattering gore.

Slate heard a crack and felt a sting in his shoulder. He whirled to find Danny throwing the bolt of his rifle for a second shot. Slate leapt across the gap between them, knocking the rifle out of Danny's hands. Danny pulled his knife and desperately plunged it into the monster's chest. The beast howled in pain and rage, and snapped its jaws on Danny's neck all but severing the head that hung backward over his shoulder by a few shreds of muscle and skin.

The sound of an engine; Cameron was in the truck. He fish hooked the pickup backward, slamming into one of the stunted pines and ground the gears jumping the truck across the clearing. Slate ran after the lurching pickup as it tore down the rutted track. When it slowed for a sharp bend, he jumped onto the bumper and threw himself into the bed. Cameron looked into the rearview mirror and saw the glittering golden eyes an instant before the truck lurched off the track and into the trees. The impact threw Slate from the bed and with a force that would have killed a human hurled him against a thick tree trunk.

Slate stood, shaking himself violently. He turned to the truck and was about to charge it when flame began licking from the underside. Fire. Danger. He warily scuttled backward in a crouch. In a few seconds, the cab was burning and soon after, the gas tank erupted in a burst of flame. The trees caught, and in a moment, the forest was on fire.

Danger. Survive. Escape. Run.

Slate ran and ran, taking every path and trail that led him away from the blaze. Had he been a little less wolf and a little more human, he might have noticed the trigger set into a path far from the cabin. The device tripped the shutter of the hidden camera that captured the Slate-wolf running headlong through the Barrens into the darkness away from the brightening light.

CHAPTER TWENTY-FIVE

Monzo sat in the office in the back of The Cricket, a cigar unlit between his fingers. He pored over the club's receipts for the second time. Business was better than ever. The Cricket was always a money laundering location for the Mob, and even if it ran in the red a little, there was no harm to the operation. But he never expected it to turn such a profit. It almost made the straight life look attractive.

Monzo was afraid that the rumors surrounding Johnny Ace's departure would scare people away from the club, but they didn't. If anything, the stories added to The Cricket's allure. Monzo didn't play the genial host as Johnny did; he didn't schmooze with the crowd. He remained aloof, but he was definitely a celebrity. People pointed him out and heads turned when he walked through the club or on those occasions when he sat at his table.

Monzo was king of his world in this time in that place, but the crown weighed heavily. Trouble erupted again between his gang and Stubbs. After a few weeks of quiet, a shootout in the Combat Zone between a group of his enforcers and Stubbs' men left three dead, one of them a civilian waiting for a bus. The newspapers screamed and so did Whelker. The cops beefed up street patrols and a half dozen of Monzo's street dealers were picked up in a sweep. It was small comfort that at least as many of Stubbs' people went down too. It made for some interesting times in the holding cell until the night sergeant wised up and separated the gangs.

Monzo's dilemma was simple. He'd used Slate the last time to bully Stubbs into cooperation. Now Slate was gone. If he called a meeting again, he wouldn't have a card to trump force and bravado. Whatever move he made next would be crucial. So far Pegg had been unsuccessful finding Slate. Whatever power he had, or force, or whatever you'd call it, was limited. And whoever set the other werewolf on them was still out there. Pegg hadn't found him yet either, and he was a bigger threat than Stubbs.

Monzo lit his cigar and leaned back in his chair. There were tough times before and he'd fought his way through them all with Eddie and Paco behind him. He liked to think that when all else failed, he could still climb over his desk and punch his antagonist in the teeth, but this time, there were some things in play that brass knuckles and bullets couldn't handle.

But there were also still some things that they could, and in that, Monzo took some comfort.

CHAPTER TWENTY-SIX

The forest fire was contained to a relatively small area partly because of the vigilance of the fire spotters and the quick response of the firemen and partly because of a thunderstorm that soaked the area around the fire and slowed its spread. Slate spent the day in hiding, watching the firemen kill the last few hot spots and pull out their equipment. His foot ached where his toes had been burned, although they were almost healed. Late in the afternoon he circled back to the clearing with the cabin. It was all a blackened ruin.

The bodies were gone, taken by the firemen, but the bodies would have been burned to their bones by the flames leaving no evidence of their savage deaths before the fire. His gear was gone as well, burned to ash in the cabin. He was all but naked in tattered jeans and there was nothing here to cover him. When the redneck brothers searched him, they missed the money stuffed into his waist band where he'd cut open a part of the inside seam. Not much, but it was something. He prodded through the ashes in the clearing with a stick and found the charred stock and twisted barrel of Danny's rifle and the exploded propane cylinder among other remnants of the catastrophe; nothing useful.

Then the stick hit something hard. Slate crouched and brushed the ashes away; Danny's Ka-Bar combat knife. He tested the edge with his thumb, remembering the scalpel-thin cut, now healed, across his thigh. Still sharp; likely the temper was ruined by the heat but he could fix that as soon as he had access to a fire and water. Suddenly things looked better.

He remembered the details of his capture, of his torture, and to his surprise, much of the detail of the transformation and the slaughter that followed. Lines were blurring between the man and the beast, fusing into one mind. And when it was done, what would he become? Slate wasn't sure he wanted to know, but he was sure that he would soon find out.

One more night, maybe two and the changes would stop for a while. The Barrens proved a good place to hide, but chance and circumstance catch up with all of us, Slate thought. In the meantime: Survive.

❖ ❖ ❖

In Camden, Bill Hanisford, the camera man hung 8 x 10 prints to dry in the red light of his darkroom. His chubby bulk crowded the work table in the makeshift lab, little more than a glorified closet in his apartment. The forest fire was a mixed blessing. The flames damaged some pretty costly equipment, but they also panicked the fauna that tripped the two hidden cams multiple times as the livestock ran from the fire. The result was dozens of night shots instead of a handful. Maybe he'd find some animal shots full of panic or pathos he could sell to some nature magazine. What he really wanted as a shot of the Jersey Devil, or something that looked like it that he could peddle to one of the tabloids or the UFO magazines. That's where the real money lay.

Lots of whitetail deer, shot after shot drying on the line. And then one unusual pic came out of the tray. Arms and legs…a man? Not quite. The proportions were a little bit askew, the arms too long, the hands too big, the legs a little bit crooked. The distant glow of the fire skewed the contrast and backlit the figure, its head turned three quarters toward the camera. Hanisford grabbed a magnifying glass and darted through the curtains of his darkroom into the light.

He peered through the glass and let out a breathless, "Holy shit." What he saw was a face covered with hair; not just bearded, but covered every square inch. In five seconds he was on the telephone.

CHAPTER TWENTY-SEVEN

Slate scavenged some ill-fitting clothes and some plastic sheeting from a hunting cabin that looked as if some local kids broke into it, used it as a party house and left with everything they could carry. Everything they couldn't carry they smashed to pieces. From the looks of the place, Slate figured the owners hadn't been back for a long time, but although the cabin offered a roof and a door, he wasn't willing to risk trading safety for comfort. That afternoon he slept in the woods nearby, the Ka-Bar knife under his hand. When he woke, the shadows were long and the sun was low. He was hungry, but in a while the change would come, and the beast would feed them both. He drank from a nearby stream, stripped and folded his clothes into a neat pile, wrapped them in the plastic sheet, and sat on the ground to wait.

❖ ❖ ❖

Moonrise.

The transformation was painful but seemed less difficult as if Slate's body were becoming accustomed to it. The night air was cool, the scent of pines tinged with wood smoke by the fire the day before. The Slate-wolf threw back his head and howled at the cold eye of moon that peered through the trees and bathed the path in ghostly light.

Hunger. Hunt.

His healing toes barely troubled him as he loped through the forest, yellow eyes searching, ears alert, nostrils twitching, searching for prey. Several klicks from the cabin he caught a faint whiff of blood. He stopped, listening, sniffing, tasting the air. Slate turned and crashed through the brush toward the source of the wind-borne scent. The further he ran, the stronger the smell of hot blood became and it mingled with an acrid animal scent. Slate burst into a clearing and in the cold moonlight found a cougar crouched over a fallen deer, its snout rooting in the deer's guts. The bloody head whirled and the cougar dropped into a snarling crouch at the rival for its kill. It hesitated, confused. Its prey looked like a man but was not. Slate also dropped into a crouch, circling the cat. The cougar snarled, its haunches flexing to spring.

The cat was easily as large as Slate and almost pound-for-pound the equal of his weight. It would be a fair fight. The cougar sprung at the same instant Slate did. The pair collided in mid-air and fell to the clearing, thrashing and clawing each other. The cougar's hind paws raked Slate's legs viciously, scoring his hide and adding his scent to the bouquet of blood. Slate rolled to the side and as he did, he slashed the cougar's face, leaving its ear hanging by bloody threads. The cougar whirled and its fangs snapped on the air as Slate's jaws bit hard, crushing the cat's foreleg.

The cougar howled in pain and rage and tried to turn fast enough to follow the beast's circling movement. Slate leapt over the cougar and it swiveled on its three good legs to meet a charge that never came. Before the cat completed its turn, Slate leapt and the cougar turned again, desperate. Slate feinted a leap. The cat began its turn and realized too late that Slate hadn't jumped and its back was exposed. Slate leapt on the cougar's back, locking his legs around the animal's torso and digging his claws into the cat's head in an unbreakable grip. With a vicious wrench, Slate twisted the cougar's head almost from its body.

Slate stood over his kill. His lungs were burning; his legs were on fire, but he felt more alive than at any moment in his life. He felt a thrill of victory as he tore open the cougar's body and gorged himself on the hot red meat. He ate its life as he ate its flesh, the essence of another hunter, another predator, and he felt power surge through him. As a man he killed many others like himself, but it was a job. He felt relief that his opponent died rather than he; he felt satisfaction in his skill, but he never felt such a rush of raw triumph before. He killed the cougar. His strategy worked. Strategy?

Slate froze. He drew back from the cougar's corpse and became still, looking at the moonlit ground. Thoughts. He had thoughts. He was aware. He was a beast, but he was aware of himself. I think, therefore I am. Away from Pegg's control, he'd become his own master.

Suddenly, Slate had choices. He tipped his head back and gazed at the Moon's impassive face. He opened his mouth, but instead of a howl came a guttural sound barely discernible as speech, but to Slate's ears, it was a symphony: "Ayar! Ayarm!"

"I am."

CHAPTER TWENTY-EIGHT

Carson Brae parked a block away from The Whisperer's town house. He was sweating as he strode through the alley, and not from the midmorning heat. He opened the back gate to see Charybdis and Scylla flanking the sidewalk like decorative statuary. Their dark eyes bored into him, turning slowly as he passed between. By the time he rang the doorbell, Brae's shirt was soaked.

The door opened and Mr. Smith grinned. His crooked teeth and caterpillar eyebrows made him look like a caricature, but Brae couldn't find him funny. "Come in, Counselor, come in." Mr. Smith bowed at the waist sweeping an arm forward with a mocking air of deference. Brae thought, straight out of T.S. Eliot: "The eternal footman holds my coat and snickers."

Through the archway of the parlor Brae saw a good-sized crate standing empty, its lid propped against the wall. Brae shuddered at the thought of what may have arrived in it. Mr. Smith followed his eyes to the crate then took his arm and aimed him at the staircase. "Nothing to concern you, Counselor. This way, please."

Mr. Smith raised his hand at the door to the Whisperer's study but before he could knock, the voice from within said, "Come."

Brae stood as before beside the armchair in front of the heavy, carved desk, waiting for the invitation to sit.

"So, Mr. Brae, what do you have to report?"

Brae wrung his hands nervously. "Where shall I begin?"

"You may begin with Mr. Monzo's pet. Has it been found?"

"Not that I've heard, Mr. Greystone, but Michael doesn't tell me everything. He's become secretive, almost paranoiac. He trusts no one except his brother Eddie, his lieutenant Paco, and that man Pegg who…"

"Yes, Pegg!" The Whisperer hissed. "That meddling fool."

"You know him?"

"Our paths have crossed before, but never directly. Pegg is a lesser talent who acquired his power by buying arcane books and artifacts. He plays at sorcery as if it were a game, a way to gratify his ego rather than a means to a greater end. He is no threat to me, but he is a proverbial thorn in my paw."

"Can you use your abilities to eliminate him?"

"Not without calling undue attention to myself from others more powerful than either of us who are inimical to my plans. Sorcery is power, but it has limits. If I use sorcery to destroy Pegg now, I will jeopardize all I that have set in motion. His time will come, and soon. Now, tell me all that you have learned."

For the next fifteen minutes, the words tumbled out of Brae's mouth with increasing speed and desperation as The Whisperer sat silent. Brae felt in his heart that the sorcerer's dissatisfaction would mean his destruction, and the longer the Whisperer was unresponsive, the shorter Brae's life became. Finally, Brae stammered his last few words, an incomplete sentence, and bowed his head. He stared at his feet waiting for the coup de grace. He shuddered, shaking a drop of sweat from his nose that mingled with a tear.

The Whisperer finally broke the silence. "This man Pegg; you must get close to him. Earn his trust. Learn what he is doing. And when the opportunity comes, kill him."

"Kill him? How?"

"He is human. Shoot him. Stab him. Strangle him. That detail does not matter. Find the means and the opportunity. I see now that I must relegate Mr. Monzo to a secondary role for the moment until you eliminate Pegg."

Granted a temporary reprieve, Brae sagged in his seat like a blow-up toy leaking air.

"Of course," said the Whisperer, "you could kill Mr. Monzo instead"

A thought ran unbidden through Brae's brain: or I could kill myself. He shuddered at the thought of what would wait for him beyond the threshold of suicide, a suicide that thwarted The Whisperer's plans.

The Whisperer dismissed him with a casual wave of his hand. "Do not fail me."

As Mr. Smith led Brae past the parlor, Brae's eyes strayed to the crate once again. Mr. Smith stopped and turned. "Not quite big enough for a man, Counselor." His eyebrows rose. "That is to say, a whole man." Mr.

"So, Mr. Brae, what do you have to report?"

Smith turned and cackling at his joke, strode to the back door as Brae stared at the crate and shuddered.

As Brae crossed the back yard of the town house, he saw the Mastiffs snap to attention. In a way he thought, they were an apt metaphor for his situation. Charybdis and Scylla; the whirlpool and the monster, The Whisperer and Monzo. Brae felt as if he'd stepped headlong into an open grave and soon the earth would cover him. If only it were that simple.

CHAPTER TWENTY-NINE

Slate spent the day sleeping off the night's exertion. When he woke, the claw marks of the cougar were healed and he was whole again. He found the way back to his camp and dressed in the shabby clothes. He remembered more about last night's transformation than any night before, but he questioned its reality. The blending of consciousness between him and the beast seemed more like a waking dream than a memory. There was one way to find out. Avoiding the trails, he carefully followed a path through the forest, letting his instinct guide him, twists and turns through the pines and the dense brush.

Something caught his attention, a scent not a sound. His head snapped up and he swiveled it from side to side, breathing deeply through his nose. Death. Blood. Meat. Slate closed his eyes and turned slowly, inhaling the scent and making it a beacon to guide him to the source. This way. He moved silently through the brush as if it were a groomed trail, following his heightened senses. In a moment he heard snarling and snuffling. In another he found the clearing and a pack of wild dogs tearing at the remains of the deer and the cougar.

The dogs turned as one from their feast, hair bristling on their backs, fangs bared, sensing a threat they didn't understand. The pack leader, a Rottweiler with a ruined eye took a step forward, a low growl rumbling from his chest. The others gathered behind him. Slate pulled his knife. The leader flexed his haunches to spring, and Slate locked eyes with him. The leader hesitated, but didn't back away. This was a fight either side might win, but at more cost than gain. Holding the leader's eyes, Slate backed away from the clearing, the Rottweiler's eyes fixed on his. Slate didn't turn until he heard the sounds of feeding and the snarling of the dogs among themselves over one bit of meat or another.

As he hiked back to his camp, Slate pondered what he learned. Last night was no dream. The hunt, the kill, the revelation; all were real. The heightened sense of smell meant that just as his human consciousness intruded on the beast's, so did the beast's on his own. Maybe it was because he and the beast were brothers under the skin; killers, hunters whose only gods were victory and survival. Whatever the reason, Slate realized that to survive he needed control and to control, he needed knowledge. Like it or not he would return to Newark before the next full moon in search of Pegg and answers.

❖ ❖ ❖

Monzo and Eddie arrived at The Cricket to find Pegg waiting in Monzo's office. Pegg sat unmoving in his chair, eyes closed. As Monzo sat behind his desk, Pegg's eyes opened, fixed on Monzo's own. Eddie started to speak, but Monzo waved him to silence.

"Mr. Pegg, how did you get in here?" Monzo said, his head tilting with curiosity. "That door is always locked."

Pegg's face formed its amused vee. "Most doors are open to me." Before Monzo could respond, Pegg said. "I believe I have found Mr. Slate." He reached over and placed a newspaper on the desk. "He's made the front page."

The newspaper was a supermarket tabloid called *The Arcane Observer*. Monzo picked it up and stared at the headline: "Jersey Devil Caught on Camera?" He stared even harder at the photograph. It was a little blurry from enlargement but if the monster it captured running through the forest was not Slate, it was a close cousin.

"The article says the photo was taken in an undisclosed area of the Pine Barrens. Unfortunately for us, that covers over a million acres of forest and wasteland." Pegg leaned back in his chair and steepled his fingers. "But on the bright side, we know which haystack has the needle."

Monzo skimmed the article that followed on an inside page while Eddie studied the picture. "You read this?" Monzo indicated the article and Pegg nodded. "As is usually the case with these publications, the details are vague and exaggeration is rampant. But there is one useful detail."

Monzo looked at the article again for a moment and back to Pegg. "And that is?"

"The photographer's name: William Hanisford. Find him and you will narrow the search to the spot where that picture was taken."

Monzo nodded. "I can see that. But what if it isn't Slate?"

Pegg smiled and drew the amulet from his pocket. "Like Frank Buck, I will 'bring him back alive,' and you'll have a new pet to show off and to protect you should Slate return."

Monzo nodded. "What do you need?"

"Your people can locate Hanisford more quickly than I. Once you find him, I will pay him a visit with a few of your more persuasive men and I believe he will show us where the picture was taken." Pegg looked to the amulet. "And I will take it from there."

CHAPTER THIRTY

In the Camden Public Library, Slate pored over the personals. In the third paper he found: Rainy Day. Have tent will travel. Count the days. In the geography section he found a topographical atlas of New Jersey and in a few minutes he located a map of the area of the Pine Barrens where he was hiding. A little calculation with the straight edge of a book spine and a pencil and paper gave him the coordinates he needed. He composed a simple personal ad using the number of letters in each word as the digits in the latitude and longitude of the general area and two words for the month and day. "None" represented zero.

Rainy Day: glad none injured—expected high mortality. Translation: Latitude 40 degrees; longitude 78 degrees; 4 September. He put the papers back on the rack and headed out the door for the post office.

CHAPTER THIRTY-ONE

Bill Hanisford whistled as he climbed the stairs to his apartment. A week ago he was broke then his Jersey Devil photo made the front page. The check from *The Arcane Observer* cleared and at least for the moment, he was flush with money. Life looked much better today than it did last week. He cradled a grocery bag and a six-pack of Michelob in his arms while he unlocked his door. No more of that bottled sheep-dip Yuengling for Bill Hanisford. He was sweating in the August heat and that cold beer looked like liquid gold. The door swung inward and he backed into the apartment, setting the bag and the beer on the floor. Hanisford threw the dead bolt and turned to find two very large men in suits sitting, one on his couch and one in his armchair. He straightened up, startled. "Who...what are you doing here?"

Neither spoke, but both rose and crossed the room so that one stood to either side of him. "Okay, if you're from Benny, tell him I have his money. I just cashed a big check." Neither of the suits spoke. "What? What?"

At that moment, the curtain across Hanisford's darkroom doorway pulled aside and Pegg strolled into the room. "Hello, Mr. Hanisford."

"Who are you?" The suits were unsettling enough, but to Hanisford the guy in the leather coat was downright scary.

"A connoisseur of fine photography who is very interested in your work."

Hanisford stammered. "What work? His head swiveled back and forth between the gangsters and settled on Pegg. "You mean the porno?"

Pegg's face folded into his amused vee. "Your nature studies, of course. Particularly this one." Pegg bought his hand from behind his back and held an 8x10 of the cover shot. "Please sit down, and let's talk." The hit men each took an elbow and steered Hanisford to the sofa. They pushed him down and sat on either side of him like bookends.

Pegg brought in a kitchen chair and sat in front of Hanisford. "Tell me, where did you take this picture?"

Hanisford hesitated. If he gave away the location, he'd lose his exclusive. "Uh, in the Pine Barrens."

Pegg turned and nodded to Leo, the thug on Hanisford's right, who clamped a dinner-plate sized hand on the photographer's thigh. The thick fingers slowly closed squeezing Hanisford's leg in a painful grip. Hanisford yelped, "I can't tell. If word gets out, everybody will know and I'll be just one more shutterboy again."

Pegg nodded at Paul on the other side who clamped a hand on Hanisford's other leg. His breath was rapid now, each pant a cry of pain. "Aaugh! Aaugh! Aaugh!" Pegg gestured with a hand and the hit men stood, yanking Hanisford's legs in the air and landing him on his back on the floor. Pegg knelt beside Hanisford's head and took off his glasses. Hanisford tried to look away but Pegg held his stare as he sorted through the darker corners of the photographer's mind.

"I'm surprised you would even set foot in the Pine Barrens, given your fear of snakes." Pegg held his right hand palm up inches from Hanisford's face. The leather sleeve of Pegg's coat began to stir and rustle and in a moment, the triangular head of a snake slithered from his cuff and into his palm. The head swayed side to side, the black beads of its eyes glistening. The tongue flicked from its mouth as it tasted the air.

Hanisford's eyes bulged and he moaned in terror. Beads of sweat stood out on his forehead like rivets on a girder. The snake's head traveled across

Pegg's fingertips and hovered an inch from Hanisford's eye. Its mouth gaped, revealing a wicked set of fangs.

"All right!" he shouted. "All right! I'll tell you."

"Pegg looked again into Hanisford's eyes and his eyelids drooped in mock pity. "No, Mr. Hanisford, you will not tell us, you will take us there." The snake retreated into Pegg's sleeve and he looked up to Leo. "Let him up, and give him one of those beers. I believe he needs one."

CHAPTER THIRTY-TWO

Slate sat with his back against the bole of a pine tree and watched the morning fog retreat as the sun rose higher over the pines. It was a roll of the dice to run the ad, but it paid off. At least one of the team was in country and coming to help him. If either of the other four saw the personal ad and the response they wouldn't run their own ads but instead wait and watch for follow-up. If his luck held, Slate wouldn't be fighting this battle alone much longer.

Survival training kept him alive and fed, but he missed the comforts of civilization enough to hitchhike to one of the nearby exits along the Interstate and get a cheap room in one of the motels that catered to over the road truckers and that took cash without asking too many questions. The need of a hot shower and the lure of a real bed under a roof were just too strong. Motel 95 was like Baby Bear's bed, just right. Not too fancy, not too crude; not too expensive, not too cheap and busy enough that one transient stopping for one night wouldn't be noticed or remembered by the management.

Behind the front desk, a surly woman sat smoking a cigarette and leafing through a movie magazine. She was lean and hard and her skin had the leathery texture you expect to find on a Carny midway shill. He gave her his only twenty and as she handed him the room key and a five dollar bill, he saw something that gave him a start on the stack of newspapers and magazines left for the guests. It was the cover of a tabloid newspaper with a full-sized picture of a werewolf, a picture of him running through the trees. He picked it up and stared at the photo and the accompanying headline for a full minute before he asked the clerk, "Can I take this with me to read?"

"That's why they're there, pal," she said around her cigarette. "But it's the latest issue, so bring it back or leave it in the room when you check out."

Slate nodded, still looking at the photo. "Sure." He folded the paper and headed for his room.

Room 108 was what anyone might expect in a cheap motel; worn carpet, cigarette burns on the furniture, a television set that got two fuzzy channels, rust stains in the sink and shower, and a mattress on the bed that felt as if a dozen baseballs were sewn up inside it. After sleeping on the ground under a bush in the rain, to Slate the place looked like Heaven.

Slate stripped off his clothes and washed them in the sink. While they hung to dry in the shower stall, he stretched out on the threadbare chenille bedspread and read *The Arcane Observer*. The article inside was typical of weekly rags like this one. It began with bold declarations of a monumental find of earth-shattering importance to the field of crypto-zoology, and the further the article went, the more vague it became until it wandered into filler material about the history of the Jersey Devil and other supernatural aspects of the Pine Barrens. Black and white drawings of the Jersey Devil swirled around the text of the article like the pages of an old pulp magazine.

William Hanisford, the photographer who caught him on camera said that it was "pure luck" that he got the picture. "I had that camera placed along one of the less used trails, and when the forest fire started, the animals stampeded away from it. The camera caught a lot of deer, but only one creature." A following paragraph recounted the fire started by a truck crash and the deaths of three local men named Tuttle.

Hanisford went on, "I plan to go back there with a full party to try to find whatever it was that tripped my camera. If it's not the Jersey Devil, it's still definitely not human and definitely not natural. But I'll be ready for him whatever I find." At the bottom of the page was a picture of Hanisford in a hunter's vest, posing with a camera in one hand and his pistol in the other. No doubt about it; Hanisford was the heavy-set photographer Slate had seen weeks before.

Slate threw the paper on the night stand and stared at the ceiling. Not only would Hanisford be trooping around the Barrens looking for the monster, as the word spread, so would every other yahoo in the state with a deer rifle and a flashlight. The next full moon was nine days away, but in the meantime he didn't want people to find him in human form any more than he did as the werewolf. He couldn't risk missing whichever of his men answered his ad, either. The fourth of September was set, and the location was right in the middle of what promised to be the biggest monster hunt in New Jersey's history. Yet there might be a way to turn the game to his advantage. His clothes would be dry in a few hours. In the meantime he planned to enjoy sheets, a mattress, and a pillow.

As he drifted off, Slate thought too that word of a werewolf in the Pine Barrens may also bring Pegg and Monzo's men. He smiled. Let them come and play in his back yard. Maybe the publicity wasn't such a bad thing after all.

CHAPTER THIRTY-THREE

Leo slapped at a mosquito on his neck and drew his hand away bloody. The Pine Barrens seemed to have every breed of bloodsucking bug in North America, and they were having a fine time biting the mobsters. The insects avoided Hanisford for the most part and Pegg completely. "How come these bugs are only biting us?"

Hanisford spoke over his shoulder. "Maybe some scent from your hair tonic or after shave. I'm not wearing any, and it seems to help. Maybe it's something in the food you eat coming through your skin." He stopped short of saying that whatever the reason, he was grateful. An hour before, Hanisford drove his Jeep as far into the forest as possible and parked it at a trail head next to several other Jeeps, pickup trucks and even a few cars. The trucks and Jeeps all had empty gun racks in their back windows.

"What's with all these trucks?" Paul said.

"Pegg looked around annoyed and turned to Hanisford. "It is a little early for hunting season, isn't it?"

Hanisford shrugged. "Monsters are always in season."

"Then we should move on before someone beats us to him."

Hanisford led them along a crooked trail through the pines. He saw boot tracks in the sandy soil, lots of them. Occasionally he heard a shout or some other sound of men, but nowhere nearby. Plenty of people were searching this part of the forest; if they ran into another party, men with guns, or a game warden maybe he could ask for help and they would give it. Surely they were out in force; a slim hope, but a hope nonetheless.

A half mile down the trail, Hanisford stepped off the trail to the left and stooped to examine the thick trunk of a pine. "Here's where we get off." Near the ground was an X blazed into the bark.

"There's no path," said Paul, looking down at his feet. His thin soled Italian-cut shoes were not designed for rough terrain and they were already scarred and muddy.

"There's a path," said Hanisford. "It's just overgrown. Follow me." He stepped off the trail and in a few seconds was all but swallowed by the brush. Leo and Paul hesitated, looking at each other for a consensus, and Pegg's cold voice snapped like a whip. "Get in there before we lose him."

A few minutes of fighting through the brush and the mobsters were sweating. Hanisford smiled to himself as he heard them cursing and complaining behind him. They were big and they were intimidating, but out here he had the edge because he knew the turf. Out of shape as he was, he could still lose them in the maze of paths and trails and get away, but then what? If he escaped and they found him again, today, next month, or in five years, they would kill him for sure, or maybe worse. He shuddered at the thought of the snake an inch from his eye. Whether he survived today or not, one shot of them would be enough for the cops, or maybe even the FBI. After all, this was kidnapping, right? A plan formed in Hanisford's mind to leave evidence to make them pay, however far they went.

Leo and Paul crashed through the dense brush like oxen, cursing as brambles snagged their suits and scored their hands. Behind them, Pegg was silent, absorbing every detail with every sense, memorizing every twist and turn of the trail. Here. Slate had been here and if he is not here now, he will be again.

Hanisford studied another blaze and led the party to his left, west judging by the sun. The brush thinned a little, and the going was easier.

"How much farther?" grumbled Paul.

"Not far now," said Hanisford. He mopped his brow with a red bandanna and tied it kerchief-style around his throat. He purposely led them in a tight curve as they neared the camera site to approach it from an intersecting trail where another camera lay hidden. As they followed the trail, Hanisford carefully stepped over the trigger to the second camera, leaving Leo to trip the shutter. "This way," he said. "We're getting close."

In a few minutes, they reached an intersection with another trail and Hanisford stopped. "This is it."

Pegg held the photo in front of him and looked around the small clearing. "And the camera?"

"Right here." Hanisford pointed to a rotting log beside the trail. He used a stick to poke around it and ensure no snakes were lurking, and then brushed away the cover of leaves and duff.

Pegg dropped to his haunches facing the direction of the camera's view. "Yes. He came from that direction," Pegg gestured with his open hand. "And he was heading that way."

"So now what?" Pegg ignored Leo's question and turned to Hanisford holding out his palm. "The film, please."

Hanisford blinked. "Film?"

"Don't be foolish, Mr. Hanisford. "After you went to such lengths to set up this camera, surely you reloaded it." Hanisford reluctantly took the film from the camera and handed it to Pegg. "We will take it back to your apartment and see, if you'll pardon the pun, what develops."

"Hello, boys." At the sound of a strange voice the four of them turned to see a khaki uniform, a campaign hat and a badge step out of the trees; a game warden. He was short, stocky and had a forehead like a boulder over a hard face that spoke of too many seasons spent out of doors. On one hip hung a walkie-talkie and on the other a .45 caliber Colt. "You fellows lost?" His hand on the .45, his thumb on the hammer, belied his offhand manner.

Hanisford stepped forward. "No, officer…" he squinted at the name tag on the uniform, "…Poston." Before Pegg could stop him he fished a card out of his vest and handed it to the warden. "My name's Hanisford, I'm a photographer." He bent down and pulled the camera from its hiding place and offered it as evidence.

"And these men?" Poston stepped back so that he could keep all four of them in view. "They're not exactly dressed for the occasion."

Pegg smiled and glibly said, "We represent *The Arcane Observer*. He drew a folded copy of the front page of the tabloid from his coat pocket and held it in front of him like a banner. "Perhaps you've seen it?"

Poston's lower lip opened slightly to the left showing clenched teeth. "Yeah, I've seen it. And so has every other gun-toting asshole for a hundred miles around. What you're telling me is you're the reason I'm out here on my day off along with every other warden, cop, and constable in the state." His cold eyes shifted to Hanisford. "You I can buy, but I'm not so sure about these three." He jerked his head at Pegg, Leo, and Paul. "Let's see some ID."

Things hung in the air for a second and no one moved. Suddenly, Poston's walkie-talkie crackled. "Elroy, this is Barnett. Come in." Poston's left hand dropped to the bulky unit hanging from his belt. Never taking his eyes off Leo, Paul, and Pegg or his hand off his pistol, Poston raised the walkie-talkie to his shoulder and pushed a button. "Poston here. Over."

"Got a problem in sector twenty-three; gunshot wound. Looks like some fool stepped on a booby trap of some kind. His foot's all torn to hell. I need your help. Over."

Poston took a long breath deciding and said, "I'll be there as quick as

I can. Over and out." He lowered the walkie-talkie to his belt and the rest of him didn't move. "I don't know what the game is here, boys, and I don't have time to figure it out right now. Don't be here when I come back." He backed away into the brush until he was out of sight and in a moment he was gone.

Hanisford let out a breath he's been holding for more than a minute. Leo snarled, "Who's Barney Fife there think he is, talking to us like that. We shoulda just shot his ass."

"Poston is no hick," said Pegg. Did you see the ring on his left hand? He was an Army Ranger. My guess is he would have killed one or both of you before you even got your guns clear. We should take his advice. I think we are done here. Mr. Hanisford, lead the way."

Back at Hanisford's apartment, he ran the film from the trail camera while Pegg watched over his shoulder, barely fitting into the darkroom with him. Outside, Leo and Paul sat like cathedral gargoyles on either end of the sofa. The camera took more than twenty pictures since it was reset. At least ten were of deer and one a black bear, but no werewolf. One caught Poston on patrol. There were other people in some of the shots too, groups of two to four hunters with rifles and shotguns at the ready and some lone stalkers, but none of the men was Slate.

Hanisford breathed a sigh of relief that he didn't try to trick the thugs and take their picture with the same camera. The weirdo in the leather coat, Pegg the others called him, would have seen it and the game would be over. He followed Pegg out of the darkroom and as they entered the living room, Leo and Paul rose from the couch. They were muddy, scratched, dotted with insect bites, and glaring at him. Oh, God, thought Hanisford. This is it.

"You have been very helpful to us, Mr. Hanisford," said Pegg. He reached into his coat and pulled out an envelope. Think of this as payment for today and a retainer for your future services. Pegg opened the envelope and rifled his thumb over a wad of hundred dollar bills. "You will find five thousand dollars here. We would like you to maintain your surveillance of the Pine Barrens, and perhaps even expand it. You know what interests us. If it appears on film again, I expect you to call us immediately and tell no one else. Of course our arrangement is, shall we say, confidential. Do we understand each other?"

Hanisford nodded his head slowly, still looking at the money. "Yeah. I got it."

"You will find five thousand dollars here."

"One more thing, Mr. Hanisford." Pegg pulled a sheet of paper from his pocket. It was a drawing similar to a police composite sketch. It showed a dark-haired man with a mustache and a scar that split his right eyebrow perpendicularly. Pegg wrote a telephone number on the envelope and handed it to him. "If you see this man in your pictures or in person, notify me and no one else."

Hanisford nodded. "Yeah. Right away. I got it."

Without another word, Pegg, Leo, and Paul walked out the door leaving Hanisford to ponder his mixed bag of luck. He was dangling on a big, sharp hook, but at least he was still breathing.

CHAPTER THIRTY-FOUR

Elroy Poston walked the perimeter of the marijuana patch, eyes on the ground, looking for anything out of place. The burgeoning patch probably belonged to the late Tuttle brothers. Too bad a forest fire didn't kill those degenerate bastards years ago. They were bad enough poaching deer, then Danny Tuttle came home from 'Nam and things got worse. The Army taught him all the wrong things, as if he'd been in the State Pen at Leesburg instead.

The shotgun shell booby trap blew most of the foot off the amateur monster hunter. He'd live, but he'd hobble the rest of his days. Poston helped Hartwell bandage the injured hunter and carry him to the Fish and Game truck then stayed behind while Hartwell took him to the Emergency Room. He crouched over the path and dug the shot-firing booby trap out of the ground with his knife. He looked it over closely. ; just like being back in 'Nam. Danny Tuttle's work for sure. The trap looked as if it were in the ground for a long time, so it wasn't set this week to bag the Jersey Devil.

Where there was one, Poston reasoned, there would be others. He'd better give a hard look for them before some other innocent party, if such a thing existed anymore, got hurt. This job was getting to be a pain in the ass.

What pissed him off more was letting those greaseballs walk. That photographer…what was his name? He pulled the business card out of his pocket. Hanisford. He looked like the real deal, but Poston never saw a photographer who didn't have at least one camera around his neck all the time. Hanisford had none. What was he doing in the middle of the Barrens with mob guys in suits? It all smelled wrong. And that other weirdo; he was just a little too quick with his story. I'll bet my next paycheck the answer's connected to this weed farm, thought Poston. Not too big a stretch. If there weren't so many idiots out here monster hunting, I'd burn this patch right now, and maybe I should anyway. Aah what the hell; phone it in to the Feds and let them deal with it.

Poston started walking the perimeter again, carefully studying the ground. What did the poet say? "Miles to go before I sleep."

CHAPTER THIRTY-FIVE

While Poston was looking for traps, Mike Haines was hitchhiking north on I-95. He could have rented a car, but he didn't want any record of his movement. He didn't fly for the same reason. He could have stolen a car, but then he'd be looking over his shoulder for cops the whole way. He could have ridden a bus, but he didn't like the confinement. Hitching gave him the best balance between anonymity and control. Any time he thought it was necessary, he could just get out and walk away, no questions asked.

Earlier in the day Haines stood at the edge of a truck stop parking lot with a cardboard sign that said simply "Home" and a carton of Marlboros and a six-pack of Budweiser in sight beside his duffel. He wore a field jacket in spite of the heat hoping that some trucker who had been in 'Nam, or one who had friends over there now would take him. He didn't have to wait long. Ed Hurley, an older guy with a son who followed his dad's example and joined the Marines, was hauling a load of textiles to Philly. Hurley didn't want the beer or smokes; what he wanted was company, someone to talk to who had made it back to give him hope that his son Robbie would come back too.

"I hate to see those draft protesters," Ed said around a toothpick that bobbed with every word and inflection. "Damn rah-rah college brats. I'd like to see any of 'em survive one day in the real world let alone in combat." He snorted, "Don't trust the President. Don't trust the government. What the hell are they talking about?"

If you only knew, thought Haines. If you only knew. He settled back in the seat and closed his eyes. It was going to be a long ride.

❖ ❖ ❖

"So, let me get this straight," Monzo said, leaning forward on his desk. "Slate's holed up somewhere in the Pine Barrens but you can't find him, but maybe it isn't Slate; maybe it's another werewolf."

Pegg nodded. "Yes to all three. The Pine Barrens is over a million acres of forest, but Hanisford's picture narrowed it down. And another detail is even more interesting. The date the picture was taken is the same date as a forest fire less than two miles away. I would guess that our furry friend was running away from the fire. I know which way he was running, and approximately what time, and that gives an idea of where he was and where he might have gone that night.

"Unfortunately for us that happened two weeks ago and by now he could be anywhere. But I believe that he has stayed in the Barrens for the time being. I sensed it. We can return when the moon is full and search for him then."

"Why wait?"

"A few reasons," Pegg said. "First, at the moment a number of locals and some outsiders are hunting the monster of Hanisford's photograph. When we parked Hanisford's Jeep, I saw license plates from six states. Their presence and the added patrols by the game wardens make it more likely we will be noticed. Also, your men are obviously not, shall we say, outdoorsmen. Further, Slate is what I thought him to be when I first saw him. He is a trained operative and looking for him on his own ground in human form could be a dangerous proposition."

Monzo pondered this for a moment. "So where does that leave us?"

Pegg pulled the medallion from his pocket and studied it. When the moon is full, this will call him to us, and I'll control him completely."

"What if you find a werewolf and it ain't Slate?" Eddie butted in.

Pegg smiled and raised his gaze from the medallion to Eddie. "Then you will have a new pet and with him you can make as many more as you need."

Monzo nodded his head and brushed an ash from his suit. "Whatever it takes. Do it."

Pegg nodded and stood to leave. "Eddie," said Monzo, "Go get Paco for me."

Though the tension between Monzo and Stubbs had eased briefly, Monzo knew that it was only a matter of time before it flared again. And if Pegg couldn't find Slate? What the hell, thought Monzo. I've gotten this far without some boogeyman on a leash. If we don't find Slate, I'll just have to deal with things the old way. But one thought gnawed Monzo's self-confidence: Monzo didn't know where Slate was but Slate knew where Monzo was. What if he came back?

Monzo opened his desk drawer and took out Vince's automatic and its empty magazine. One by one he thumbed the silver bullets into it and slipped the magazine into the pistol. He pulled back the slide, chambering a round and thumbed down the hammer. I'm not superstitious, he told himself, just pragmatic. If Slate comes, I'm ready for him.

CHAPTER THIRTY-SIX

Mr. Smith drove the Cadillac through the Southside ghetto, aware that although he saw almost no one, he was being watched from every window and doorway. The big sedan wove through block after block of tenements and burned-out buildings heading for Stubbs' headquarters behind a club called the Eight Ball. He was expected, otherwise, he would have been ambushed three blocks into the neighborhood. He pulled the Cadillac into the lot next to the club and opened the door, leaving the engine idling. He put his hands at ten and two on the steering wheel, looked straight ahead and waited.

Almost immediately, two of Stubbs' men came through a side door, one, a tall coffee colored man in a suit and the other a short round man as dark as onyx carrying a sawed-off shotgun. The tall man stepped around to Mr. Smith's door while his partner stood at the passenger side where he commanded a good aim through the window.

The tall man spoke. "You Smith?"

Mr. Smith turned his head toward him and showed a few crooked teeth in an amused smile. "Yes. That would be me."

"Get out the car." As Mr. Smith stepped out of the Cadillac, the short man came around the hood, keeping the muzzle of the shotgun leveled at his torso.

Mr. Smith raised his hands and stood still while the tall man patted him down. Smith turned his head to the short man and said, "You know, if you shoot me with that gun, you'll spray a bit on your friend here."

Shorty snorted. "Punkin balls don't spray, whitebread."

"Quite so," said Mr. Smith, and said nothing more.

As the pair led Mr. Smith to the door, he looked back to the still idling Cadillac.

"Don't worry. It'll still be here when you come back out. That is, if you come back out." The short man snickered, and Mr. Smith unnerved him by chuckling too. The door opened before them and Mr. Smith and his escorts stepped from the shade between the buildings into the deeper shadows of the nightclub.

The thugs took Mr. Smith across the empty dance floor, past a short man with a mop and past a bar gaudily lit with glowing neon beer signs. Behind the bar a barrel-shaped man with a gleaming bald head polished glassware. He showed a gold front tooth in a grin as the trio walked past, perhaps in greeting, perhaps savoring some private joke about the impending fate of the newcomer.

The tall man opened a door at the end of the bar and led Mr. Smith into a windowless backroom stacked with beer cases and liquor crates. In its center was a table with a chair on either side. A shaded overhead light cast a dim pool in the middle of the table.

"Have a seat." The short man pushed Mr. Smith into his chair by the shoulder. Mr. Smith chuckled. "Something funny?" said Shorty.

Mr. Smith turned his head toward him and said, "Yes. As a matter of fact there is."

"Just so you know, white boy, I'm gonna enjoy driving your Caddy."

A door opened at the other end of the store room and Mardi Gras Stubbs swaggered into the room. Today Stubbs wore a midnight blue suit with a white silk shirt open at the collar, the points spread over his lapels. His fedora was tilted over one eye. A ring that was easily a full ounce of gold with two diamonds sparkled on his left pinky.

He sat opposite Mr. Smith and stared at him for a full minute. Mr. Smith met his gaze, unmoving. After dealing with Himself, Mr. Smith found Stubbs to be an amateur at best.

Finally Stubbs spoke. "So, Smith, you having hard times, or do you always dress like that?" Stubbs' henchmen snickered.

Mr. Smith turned his palms up in a form of shrug. "Unlike so many, Mr. Stubbs, I disagree that clothes make the man. Looks deceive, as do words. It is action that defines us all."

"Action, huh? So what kind of action you have in mind?"

"We have an adversary in common, a Mr. Monzo." Smith raised his eyebrows.

Stubbs eyed him warily. "How so?"

"I represent someone who would like to see Mr. Monzo's empire fall, as I am sure you would as well. Business interests aside, I understand you have other reasons for wishing ill of him;an incident at a baseball field?"

Stubbs bristled and he took in a slow breath. "I'm listening."

"My employer..."

"Hold it right there." Stubbs raised a hand in a stop gesture. "Who is your employer?"

"All in good time, Mr. Stubbs. All in good time. As I was saying, my employer would like to work with you to, shall we say, topple Mr. Monzo's empire and share the benefits."

"Share? And what's my share of all this? More important, what's his share?"

"He gets Mr. Monzo's drug trade, his numbers operation, his extortion; all of his business and you get to continue your operation unimpeded plus some expansion across Prospect into the North side."

"And to make this work, what do I have to do?"

"You have men and guns and you can recruit more." He smiled crookedly. "You will provide, shall we say, the muscle."

"And what do you provide?"

"The edge, Mr. Stubbs, the edge." Stubbs stared at him and Mr. Smith continued. "You've noticed, I'm sure, a change in this city. Things are happening that simply cannot be explained like Mr. Monzo's, shall we say, new enforcer? We can make them happen too."

Stubbs pondered this thought for a moment and threw back his head and laughed. "I thought you were crazy for coming here all by yourself, and now I know you are." He looked over Mr. Smith's shoulder and said. "Shorty, Junior, take Quasimodo here someplace quiet and leave a message for his boss, if he really has one." He leveled his gaze at Mr. Smith's face. "That Caddy of yours gonna have a new hood ornament, Smith. You got my word."

Mr. Smith smiled again and affably spread his hands. "Last chance to take the offer, Mr. Stubbs."

Stubbs' eyes blazed for a second and then he threw back his head and laughed again. "I must admit, Smith, you got some balls on you." Stubbs' face became hard and he snarled through clenched teeth, "Get his ass out of here."

Junior and Shorty stepped forward and Mr. Smith raised his hand before his face. The runic sigil carved into its back began to glow a dull yellow at first, then a deep red. Stubbs' face took on a puzzled look. "What..."

Shorty cried, "Boss, I can't see! My eyes... can't see a damned thing!"

Junior rubbed at his face. "I can't see either!"

"Nicely symbolic, don't you think?" Mr. Smith cackled. "It perpetuates the metaphor of men with no vision. You had your chance." Stubbs stared wide eyed and unseeing, as if the light had gone out in the windowless room.

Junior panicked and pulled a revolver from his waistband and fired at the sound of Mr. Smith's voice, but Mr. Smith was already headed for the door. Junior's shot hit Shorty in the chest. Shorty's finger jerked on the trigger of his shotgun and blew Junior backward into a stack of crates.

The door burst open and men with guns stormed into what seemed to be a pitch black room. "Nobody shoot! Nobody shoot!" yelled Stubbs. The darkness licked like tendrils of smoke around the doorway and spread, darkening the dance floor as Mr. Smith casually strolled to his waiting Cadillac, whistling "Round Midnight." Stubbs and his men ran to the parking lot in time to see the Caddy's tail lights turn a corner two blocks up the street and disappear.

Stubbs stared after the car, realizing that he just made one big-assed mistake. He turned to his men and said, "I've had enough of this voodoo shit. Get Monzo on the phone. Now."

CHAPTER THIRTY-SEVEN

"Greystone," said Pegg. "His name is Greystone. As soon as Stubbs described Mr. Smith, I knew who was at work here."

"Who and what exactly is he?" asked Monzo.

"Greystone is a wizard. He's something of a rogue; he doesn't like playing by the rules."

"Rules?" said Eddie, "What rules?"

Pegg drew in a long breath for what promised to be a long explanation. "Rules. Yes, even hell has rules." He turned his face from Eddie to Monzo. "You and Mr. Stubbs follow a set of operating principles, a code of sorts to prevent unnecessary conflict and even mutual destruction; what gang runs what street, where the police can and can't go, what warrants reprisal and what does not. Is that not so?"

Monzo nodded. "If you want to put it that way, yeah, we have rules."

"Wizards likewise must behave according to certain 'protocols' is a good word. We have rules; the primary difference being that to ignore them puts not only the individual in peril or as in your case an operation or base of power. Our breaking those rules can upset things on a much grander scale. Like your empire, our success depends largely on the things unseen and on keeping them unseen. One of the greatest strengths of magic is the willful refusal of most people to believe in it. They hide their heads like ostriches, and so long as they can convince themselves that it is a fantasy, they are complacent and those like myself can function unimpeded.

"Take your operation as an analogy; so long as you operate under the radar, the public is perfectly happy to ignore you and pretend that you do not exist, but when incidents happen like the recent shootouts, beheadings, and other lurid crimes, they are forced to see and their complacency is shattered. Then they take up their torches and pitchforks and march on City Hall demanding it all be stopped."

"I see where you're headed with this," said Monzo. "But what about this Greystone? Can't you take him off the board?"

"I can locate Greystone with a little effort. I imagine he knows where I am at this moment. In theory I could uproot a mountain and drop it on him, or have a crater open in the earth and swallow his house, or destroy him in any number of exotic ways, and he could do the same to me, but to do so would call unwanted attention from a public that wants to disbelieve. That spotlight of attention would find its way to practitioners far more powerful than I who value their secrecy and they would not be pleased. History would repeat itself, and the torches and pitchforks would be literal."

"Then can't these higher powers take him out?" Monzo found himself fascinated with the machinations of a power structure so far beyond his own.

"I wish it were so simple." Pegg stared out the window past Monzo's shoulder. "Magic is a whole cloth. To use magic to destroy magic tears a piece from it, upsets balances far beyond our petty world and such tears are slow to heal. This is why wizards employ human agents, to prevent such destructive conflicts between them, like Greystone used his minion to visit Stubbs. Greystone is mortal; a human could kill him, although his protection would make it very difficult."

"And you as well?"

Pegg's eyes locked onto Monzo's. "Yes, I as well." A simple statement of fact; no challenge, no fear. "We are all mortal, but none of us would willingly destroy another."

"But I can take out a hit on Greystone." Monzo smiled as the two worlds finally became tangent.

"That is a possible course, but not an easy one. He will be well protected."

"You find him," said Eddie, "and we'll take it from there."

"There may be one other detail we have to address," said Pegg. "The late Vince was most likely in Greystone's employ. If Greystone had one spy in your camp, there may be others. You must all be extremely careful of what is said and to whom."

Monzo took a long pull on his cigar. "All of my men have been with me for years. A lot of them are family."

"Vince was probably a simple matter of greed, as you said yourself. I would guess he was recruited by Greystone's henchman Mr. Smith and never met Greystone face-to-face, but magic can turn the most loyal head through fear if not desire. I would trust no one outside your closest circle."

"Assuming this Greystone has a spy in my camp, could you find him?"

"Possibly. Vince gave no outward sign, but I could detect no magic at work in him. He was just a hired gun. If Greystone is manipulating someone through magic, I would know it, unless, of course, Greystone has employed a cloaking spell."

"And you're not always here."

"No, but there are certain things that I can do to protect you when I am not. I could bring in some of my people…"

"No." Monzo's tone was preemptory. He stared hard at Pegg. "No outsiders. If I can't trust my own men, I can't trust yours either. You do what you can and I'll take my chances."

"Fair enough," said Pegg.

"Take Leo and Paul since they've been there before." He turned to Paco. "You go too." Paco's eyes widened. He opened his mouth to speak and Monzo raised one finger. "I don't want any screw-ups, and I need Eddie here."

Pegg nodded and stood. "Now if you'll excuse me, I have two people to find."

CHAPTER THIRTY-EIGHT

Carson Brae pulled his Mercedes up to the factory gate, flashed his headlights, and blew three blasts on his horn. The gate ratcheted back and he drove inside. Beads of sweat ran down his back and dotted his upper lip. The whole scene had spiraled out of control. Kill Pegg or kill Monzo. Either way he would die, but at least he wouldn't suffer through eternity at the hands of those things, those horrors from his psyche. He drove up to the building entrance where two of Monzo's thugs were waiting. He was expected, and they didn't pat him down or search his briefcase. One of them led him inside and upstairs to Monzo's office. Brae screwed up his courage, put on his best courtroom face, and stepped into the lion's den.

Monzo sat, hands folded, behind his desk as usual but Eddie was absent. Instead, Frankie sat in a chair by the door. Brae looked around as he sat. Pegg was not there. The choice was made for him. "Hello, Michael. Where's Eddie?"

"Eddie's on an errand, Carson." Monzo smiled. He gestured with his chin. "You brought your briefcase. You have papers for me to sign?"

Brae nodded, a little too quickly. "Yes, some tax forms for The Cricket." He unconsciously rubbed the back of his hand. It had started to itch the moment he sat down and the itch was getting stronger.

"No rush. I was about to have a drink when you came. Would you like one too? Frankie, fix us both a bourbon, neat. You'll be glad to know that I heard from Stubbs. We won't be warring anymore."

Brae nodded and forced a smile. "That's good news, Michael. I'll tell Whelker. He'll be relieved." The itching was worse and was crossing the line into the pain zone.

"Remember what you said to me about Ockham's Razor?"

Brae nodded. "Yes, the simplest answer to a problem is most likely correct."

"Turns out you were wrong. Seems my mystery man exists after all. His name is Greystone."

Brae's eyes twitched, but he kept his game face. "Can't say I've ever heard of him."

"Well, you won't have to concern yourself with him. Where dealing with him is concerned, the simplest solution is the right one, and that's being taken care of even as we speak."

Frankie set the drinks on Monzo's desk but didn't sit down. Instead, he stood behind Brae's chair to the side, his hand in his coat.

"Drink up, Carson. For old times' sake."

Brae reached for the drink and his skin turned hot. Monzo unfolded his hands revealing a thin band of silver Pegg had carved with runes on his left middle finger. He slowly moved his hand across the desk toward Brae's, and the closer it came, the greater the heat. Monzo lunged forward to grab Brae's wrist and the sigil the Whisperer had carved in it burst into flames through his skin. Frankie and Monzo both leaped back, startled by the sudden flare.

Brae's eyes bulged in pain and horror. It was now or never. He plunged his burning hand into the briefcase and pulled out a snub-nosed pistol. Brae got off one shot before Monzo fired two of the silver bullets from Vince's automatic into his chest and Frankie put one in the back of his head. Brae slumped to the floor on his back, the revolver clutched in the charred ruin of his hand.

Monzo stood over Brae and shook his head sadly. "Of all people, Carson." Brae stared up at the ceiling as the light dimmed, and in the distance, he saw a deeper darkness and heard the gibbering and shrieking of the demons that awaited him.

CHAPTER THIRTY-NINE

Across town, three of Monzo's men, faces masked, waited in the alley behind The Whisperer's brownstone. Eddie and two others were parked on the street with a clear view of the front door. There was movement behind the curtains. The targets were home. In the alley one of the masked men tried the gate and was surprised to find it open. The trio crept into the walled yard, and the gate swung shut behind them. They stepped quietly along the walk toward the house and were halfway there when a low growl sounded from a dark corner of the yard. The thugs turned toward the sound.

"Dog," whispered one, cocking the hammer of his automatic. At that instant, Charybdis lunged from behind them, tearing out the man's throat. Scylla sprang at a second man, knocking him to the ground and sinking her fangs into the forearm he raised to protect his face. The third man put the muzzle of his silenced pistol to the back of Charybdis' head and fired two shots into the mastiff's brain. It slumped over its victim's body and joined him in death. He turned to fire at Scylla at the same instant that found her sinking her fangs into his thigh. He panic-fired shot after shot into the dog's body and finally it shuddered and died. The silver bullets worked, but not fast enough. He had to pry the mastiff's jaws from his leg. Hot blood pumped from his wound. The bitch had hit an artery.

He was within throwing distance of the house. The best he could do was to try for a window. He pulled the pin on a phosphorous grenade and pitched it. He smiled at the tinkling of broken glass and blacked out.

In a moment, the town house was ablaze from top to bottom. Windows exploded outward and flames roared from the empty casements. Eddie's men sighted their rifles on the front of the house. No one came out the front door. No one came through the windows. "Time to go," Eddie said. He gunned the motor and pulled around into the alley. No one waited outside the gate. Eddie and his men ran into the yard and saw the carnage lit by the hellish glow of the fire. Each grabbed a body, dead or alive, and dragged them through the gate to the car as they heard the wail of the first siren.

❖ ❖ ❖

Down the block, The Whisperer watched as the firemen desperately tried to prevent the fire from spreading to the nearby houses. "That fool Monzo; this debt will not go unpaid," he hissed.

Beside him, Mr. Smith simply nodded his head in silence.

CHAPTER FORTY

Four a.m. September fourth found Mike Haines in New Jersey stepping out of the cab of a tractor-trailer in the middle of nowhere. He'd been watching the mile markers carefully and when he saw the closest one to Slate's coordinates, he told the driver to pull over.

"What's the matter," Tom, the driver said, slowing the rig. "You gonna be sick?"

"No," said Haines. "This where I get off."

Tom blinked. "There's nothin' here but trees, man. Not even an access road." The rig glided to a stop on the berm. "Everything okay?"

"Haines smiled and nodded his head. "Couldn't be better. This is where I want to be." He pulled out his bag and reached into his pocket. He handed a hundred dollar bill to Tom. "Thanks again, Tom. You never saw me."

"Okay," said Tom. He looked at the bill in his hand and when he looked up, Haines was gone.

Haines hopped the guardrail and immediately jumped from civilization into absolute wilderness. A hundred yards into the forest and the last trace of the highway was the sound of an occasional truck. Even in the dark Haines could sense the complete concealment the Pine Barrens offered. No lights behind; no stars overhead. Slate chose his hideout well. Out of sight from the road, Haines snapped on a flashlight and looked around. In a few minutes he found a tree with heavy limbs and a crotch that would support his weight. He easily climbed it and pulled his duffel up with him.

Settled in the tree, he pulled a .45 automatic from his jacket, set it in his lap and closed his eyes, not to sleep but to listen. He had slept enough in the truck. It would be daylight in a few hours, and then he could start looking for landmarks.

CHAPTER FORTY-ONE

Slate spent his night carefully picking his way along the trails that led to the rendezvous point. A little light from the waxing moon filtered through the pines and showed him enough to find his way. It was a ten click hike to the spot; he'd stayed clear of it for several days to avoid drawing attention. He wanted to arrive at a vantage point where he could conceal himself before daybreak and watch the area. His heightened senses picked up sounds and scents of the forest at night. Stealthy footsteps, startled crashing through the brush in escape, the snarl of a predator and the thud of its prey on the ground. The scent of pines tweaked his nostrils along with the aroma of hot blood and raw meat on the night breezes. Just as the man intruded on the beast, so did the beast intrude on the man.

Slate reached his destination without incident just before dawn. The red sky portended rain, but he smiled at the thought that the tent would soon arrive.

❖ ❖ ❖

Haines' eyes snapped open at the faint sound of a footstep below him. Looking down from the tree, he saw a big man in jeans and a hunting vest with a "gimmie" hat that said "Cat Diesel Power" cocked back on his head. A braid of thick blond hair hung to his shoulders. He carried a Marlin 30.06 at port arms and looked at first glance like any other local hunter. His boots gave him away, though; jungle boots designed to protect the feet but allow sweat and water to evaporate to prevent fungus and jungle rot.

When he was directly under the tree, Haines gave a sharp three-note whistle, the sound of a bird, but not a bird. The man below halted and whistled in return.

"Welcome to the Pine Barrens, Swede. Right on time."

The big man looked up and grinned through a thick beard at Haines. "You know me. Never miss a show. Your tent?"

"My tent." Translation: I placed the response ad. "Catch." Haines threw his bag to Swede and dropped lightly to the trail. "What's with the pony tail? You look like my kid sister."

Swede grinned again, showing a gold canine. "Naah, beard's in the wrong place." He chuckled. "When in Rome, Mikey. I like to blend in with the hippies. Don't get much peace, but I get all the love I can handle." He handed Haines the duffel. "Let's move out."

"One minute." Haines opened his bag and pulled out an Ithaca shotgun broken down for travel. In a moment he had it loaded and in working

"Welcome to the Pine Barrens, Swede."

order. Swede looked around him. "This is some weird ass scenery. Never saw anything quite like it."

Haines shrugged. "When you come right down to it, Swede, it's just another jungle." He pulled a compass from his pocket. He oriented it, studied his map for a moment and pointed. "The way I figure it, we have to go about eight klicks linear, and judging by the features on the map, we'll do better to skirt this hill." He pointed to an elevation on the map. "It's no great height but we'll stay out of sight easier if we walk around it; better cover." He jerked his thumb. "Walk this way."

The pair followed a deer trail for a little over an hour through the pines and brush. As the haze burned off, the mosquitoes began to swarm and so did the deer flies. Swede swore as he slapped at one of the biting flies on the back of his hand. "I thought Deet was good for just about anything that flew and bit," he grumbled. "Says so on the tube."

"I guess Jersey flies can't read."

Swede and Haines stepped into a rare clearing. Haines pulled out the map and the compass. "We turn seven degrees west here and…" He stopped. "Hear that?"

"Yeah," said Swede a second later. "Chopper."

As one, Swede and Haines dove into the brush and in a moment the copter passed over the clearing. Swede stood to follow it, a hand over his eyes. "Dammit. He's turning. He's coming back."

The chopper hovered low over the clearing for a moment as if the pilot planned to land, the wind from its rotors scouring the clearing and raising dirt and duff in a cloud. It was an old Bell Iroquois with civilian markings. The side door opened and a ladder snaked out, reaching almost to the ground. A figure with a rifle and a pack slung over his shoulders swung through the door and shinned down the ladder. He looked around quickly and gave an "all clear" signal to the pilot. The chopper rose and turned south, trailing the ladder with it.

The newcomer had a bodybuilder's shape, short and stocky with broad shoulders and a thin waist under a tight jacket. His short hair and ears made him for a classic Jarhead. Swede gave the whistle and the passenger froze. He whistled in return. Swede stood up and said, "Bang, you're dead."

Haines stepped from his cover and said, "That was really subtle. You always did know how to make an entrance, Singer."

Singer grinned. "What can I tell you? I just spotted the message two days ago in Omaha, and I didn't want to miss the show." Singer shrugged out of his knapsack. "Glad we're all still ambulatory." He shrugged out of his pack. "Well, I didn't run the ad, and since you two are together and heading for the same spot I am, I'm guessing neither of you did either. That leaves Slate."

"Unless we're being gamed by the Company," said Haines.

"There is that possibility," said Singer, "but to do that they'd have to know the codes, and I don't think there's a man alive could make Slate give it up, or any of us either."

"But we'd still better be careful," Swede chimed in. "Speaking of which, we'd better haul ass out of this spot in case somebody besides us saw the chopper drop you off."

Without another word, Haines set off into the brush and Swede and Singer fell in behind.

CHAPTER FORTY-TWO

A few klicks away, Slate waited. He had given a lot of thought to how he would tell his men what they must know. The last time he changed, he focused on keeping his identity and maintaining control. He couldn't stop the change, but he could restrain himself from running wild. A trick he'd learned years before from a shaman in Cambodia, to visualize a stone figure of himself, fixed, unmoving at the center of his being, made it possible for him to focus and to keep from breaking loose. As long as he could hold that figure in his mind, he could control himself the same way he did under torture, but sudden noises and other distractions could still take his inner eye away and the allow the beast to take over.

On the ground beside him lay the chains from the cabin's a-frame. They may not be necessary but were a safeguard nonetheless. The team needed to see the change happen firsthand to understand what he had become before he asked them to go with him after Pegg and Monzo. He didn't think they would refuse him, but they deserved the option.

In the valley below he placed two short stakes, each with a scrap of cloth from his shirt, one slightly higher than the other. Sighting from the taller one over the shorter would send them in the right direction.

Slate watched the sun climb the sky. Noon came and went. A party of hunters crashed through the brush in the next valley. A herd of deer ran swift and silent past his covert. Then his eye caught the slightest movement below him. He strained his eyes and saw at the fringe of the trees a lone figure step out of the green shadows. He could tell even at a distance it was Singer. For a few minutes he walked the area, looking at the ground, and paused when he found the first stake. In a moment, he located the second one and stood facing Slate's direction.

Singer pulled up the stakes, covered them with duff and began walking north. Although he couldn't see or hear Haines and Swede, Singer knew they were flanking him fifty meters or so to either side. Overhead, the sky began to cloud up ahead of a thunderstorm, a mixed blessing. A storm would cover their tracks, but also make it harder to hear an approaching enemy. In the plus column, deer flies don't swarm in the rain. He started the climb from the shallow valley and a few meters into the trees heard the three-note whistle. Singer stood still and whistled in reply. Whistles came from either side of him and a voice said, "Olly olly oxen free." Swede and Haines joined Singer and in a moment Slate came out of a stand of stunted pines. "Glad you all came. Have I got a story to tell you guys."

CHAPTER FORTY-THREE

Miles away, the white Econoline van bounced along a rutted track through unending ranks of pines. Branches and brush raked the sides of the van as it lumbered toward a point on the map in Pegg's head. Paco was driving and his mood grew more tense by the minute. The sky had opened up and dumped the heaviest rain they had ever seen. Twice, the reinforced van had dragged bottom, forcing Leo and Paul to get out and push. Their mood was no better than Paco's; they rode in the back in the compartment designed to hold Slate. "So, Pegg," said Leo, "If we catch the werewolf, and we put him in here, where do Paul and I ride?"

Pegg turned in the seat and smiled. "You ride back there with him, of course. Or I suppose you could ride on the roof, but given how rough the ride is, you would probably fall off." He paused a beat, enjoying the incredulous stares of the two mobsters. "We will keep Mr. Slate in the back until he is human again. You can tie him up to your satisfaction, and then you can all enjoy the ride together." By the looks on their faces, Pegg could see that neither was satisfied with the arrangement.

"How much further, Pegg?" Paco said, peering through the gunmetal downpour.

"Not far, Paco, not far at all." Pegg leaned back and closed his eyes. Their end point was not far at all in terms of distance, but it would take quite a while at the rate they were going to get there.

CHAPTER FORTY-FOUR

"**A**nd that's the story." Slate finished the can of Budweiser that Haines gave him. "Damn, that was good; got another one of these?" Haines dug in his pack and threw another can to him. Rain pounded the tarp over their improvised lean-to.

"So let me get this straight," said Singer. "You turn into an honest to goodness werewolf; fangs, fur, the whole bit?"

Slate nodded. "That's the fact."

"And you're super strong?" asked Haines.

"I wouldn't call it super, but I'm a hell of a lot stronger than usual."

"Damn," said Swede. "Anybody else told me that story, I'd figure he was dropping acid."

"I'd be right there with you, Swede," said Slate taking a pull from the beer. "Except that I've got first-hand experience. What time is it?"

Swede looked at his watch. "Seventeen-thirty-seven."

"Stick around for few more hours, chain me to that tree over there, and you'll see it all for yourself."

"And what about these mob guys who did this to you?" said Haines.

"We'll talk about that in the morning. First, I want you to see what you're getting into. I owe you that."

Swede snorted. "Somebody does something to one of us, he does it to all of us." The others nodded. "You've saved all our lives more than once, Johnny. We owe you that."

There was a long uncomfortable silence then Slate looked up at the sky. "I hope the rain quits. If it doesn't, my fur'll stink like a Saigon hooker."

"As if that would change anything," quipped Singer.

Swede laughed first, breaking the tension, and one by one the others joined in. Business as usual.

CHAPTER FORTY-FIVE

"**W**e are here," said Pegg. The van pulled into a good-sized clearing. A rusted pickup truck and a bottle green Jeep were parked side by side. Ruts and tire tracks filled with water showed how busy the spot had been the past week or so.

"Here? Where?" said Paco. "There's nothing here but trees."

Pegg turned to Leo and Paul. "Do you recognize this place?"

Leo peered through the windshield and the rain. "Looks like the place that camera guy took us to."

Pegg turned back to Paco. "Here, Paco, is where."

"Now what?" said Paul.

"Now," said Pegg, closing his eyes, "we wait. In a few hours the moon will rise, rain or shine, and we start hunting."

CHAPTER FORTY-SIX

The rain quit a little before sunset, and it left the forest dripping. "This tree will do," said Slate throwing the chains at the roots of a thick pine.

"You told us you could control yourself when you changed, said Haines. Do you really need the chains?"

"My control is still shaky at best. I don't want to take chances at this point. Who knows what might set me off. The moon'll be up soon; let's do it."

The team hacked a few branches away from the trunk of the pine and wrapped the chains tightly around the tree and Slate's torso. "Sorry I don't have a padlock."

"Got the next best thing," said Swede. He pulled three stainless steel carabiners from his knapsack and snapped them into place through the chain links. "Those should hold the chains all right."

"Okay guys. Stand back. It's coming."

Moonrise.

"All right, gentlemen, let's go." Pegg opened the passenger door of the van and stepped outside into the cool, damp night air. He slid back the side door and Leo and Paul climbed out, grumbling and stretching their stiff muscles. Paco came around the front of the van with a heavy bag.

"Paco has weapons for you," said Pegg. "Leave yours in the van. Slate will be in werewolf form when we find him, and you already know that ordinary bullets aren't effective." Paco handed a compressed air dart gun to Leo, and a .45 automatic to Paul. He pulled a cut-down riot gun from the bag and began loading it with shells filled with silver shot. "You said 'when' we find Slate. Don't you mean 'if'?"

Pegg raised his eyes to the tatters of cloud brightening by the second as the moon rose. "I meant 'when,' Paco." He reached into his coat and pulled out the medallion. The purple gemstone glowed with eerie phosphorescence. "I believe this will lead me to him."

Though the mobsters were better dressed for a wilderness trek this time, the clinging rain soon had them all soaking wet and cursing every step. Their feet squished in their work shoes and every bush or bough they touched dropped a miniature shower on them. It seemed they walked half the night, though it was less than an hour when Pegg stopped. He held the amulet in front of his face and slowly turned completely around in the path. "Slate is close. This way, and be quiet."

CHAPTER FORTY-SEVEN

When the change began, the team stared in amazement. Knowing what was coming still didn't prepare them for what they would see. The change was painful, but Slate weathered it much more easily than he had before. He kept his mind fixed on the stone figure of himself, his inner persona, and the pain became remote, almost abstract as it did when Pegg used the amulet. His instinct was to fight against the chains that bound him to the tree, but by sheer force of will, he held himself still. He could see the team standing before the tree, staring at what he'd become. He sensed no fear in them but rather but a healthy wariness of the dark forces that could make this happen. It was a wariness mixed with outrage at what had been done to their leader.

Slate's ears twitched. Movement; the scent soon followed. Men were coming. He wriggled inside the chains to free his left forearm. The team stiffened. Slate slowly shook his head. He pushed his forearm through the chains and made a diagonal downward sweep with his open hand. No response. He signaled again. Singer caught on first. "Cover?" he almost whispered. Slate nodded slowly and repeated the signal. Of one mind, Singer, Haines and Swede doused their lights and scattered into the brush in three different directions.

The men were coming closer. Slate sensed four of them, and something else, the amulet. Pegg had come. Slate's mind raced as he fought panic. No, he thought. The image; see the image. He turned his mind inward and gazed at the stone icon in the distance, bringing it closer. Must think. Must think. Close my eyes. Look in not out. Trust my senses. Don't look at Pegg.

The footsteps came closer, closer, stopped twenty feet away. Slate's nose told him the hunters had arrived.

Pegg stepped toward the moonlit tree with Leo to his left and Paco and Paul to his right. The chains would make a good dart shot tricky, but Pegg hardly felt that would be necessary. "Mr. Slate, you have made this almost too easy." He raised the amulet and began to speak in his secret voice.

Slate squeezed his eyes shut. The amulet called to him, stronger with every heartbeat. Pegg's words swirled in his head: "Open your eyes. Gaze upon the stone." Slate felt his will slipping, slipping. His eyelids fluttered, and he knew in an instant he would open them.

A sharp crack sounded from the brush and the medallion flew from Pegg's hand. Suddenly free from its influence, Slate's outrage took over. He strained at the chains, and one by one, the carabiners snapped . Paul spun toward the sound of the gun and a shot from another direction made a small hole in his fore head and a big one in the back of his skull. A third shot hit Leo in the chest.

Slate roared in rage and shook away the chains. As he charged forward, Paco fired. Slate reeled. The pain was terrible, almost paralyzing. He roared in hurt and rage and staggered forward toward Pegg as Paco racked another shell. Before he could pull the trigger, Paco's face disappeared in a red spray from a shotgun blast.

Slate straightened and fixed his gaze on the wizard. For the first time since they had met Slate saw fear in his eyes.

❖ ❖ ❖

The Barrens had been quiet for several days since the Jersey Devil hoax died down, but that changed in a heartbeat. Poston's head snapped up at the sound of gunfire. Now what? He grabbed the radio from his belt and keyed it. "Poston here. I just heard shots fired north of sector sixteen. Going to investigate. Over."

"This is Barnett. Wait for backup, Elroy. Proceed to trail head sixteen B. I'll send Simmons and Balzer to meet you there."

Like hell, thought Poston. "I read you, Tom. Over and out." Poston checked the rounds in his Colt. Sixteen B was south; Poston headed west, the direction of the gunfire.

CHAPTER FORTY-EIGHT

Pegg stared in terror as the werewolf shambled unsteadily toward him, fangs dripping bloody froth. He tried to focus, to mouth a spell, but the throbbing pain in his hand nauseated him. He felt as if he might pass out. Slate wrapped a paw around Pegg's face and dug in his claws. He drew his hand back for a killing blow when suddenly his knees weakened, his eyes rolled back in his head and he slumped to the ground. Pegg began an incantation but stopped short at the feel of a 12-gauge muzzle at the base of his skull. Pegg heard the click of the hammers. "Any more tricks, wizard, and I'll do a beaut. I'll make your friggin' head disappear. Gag him and cover his eyes." Haines held the shotgun at Pegg's head while Singer bound, gagged, and blindfolded the wizard.

Swede crouched over Slate. "He's breathing, but he's hurt pretty bad."

Haines jacked a shell out of Paco's gun. He pried open the end of the shell with his knife and spilled the shot into his palm. "Silver."

"What's that mean?" said Singer.

"From every movie I ever saw, silver is fatal to a werewolf." His voice took on a tone of urgency. "We've got to get it out of him as fast as we can."

Swede pointed to Pegg. "What about him?"

Haines thought for a second, picked up the dart gun, and fired a dart into Pegg's thigh. Pegg's body went slack. "He'll keep." He leaned over Slate's body. "Swede, hold him down. Singer, shine your flashlight on him." He took a long breath and drew out his boot knife. "I sure as hell hope we're done before he comes to."

Haines was no stranger to battlefield triage. He'd cut slugs out of dozens of men in the field including Slate and had even cut one out of his own thigh, but treating a multiple gunshot wound on a werewolf was a new game. Bloody patches in the fur gave a general location to the wounds, but the fur made the buckshot holes hard to find. Further, the thick skin that sprouted that fur was like cutting harness leather.

By the time he was done Haines had cut eight pellets out of Slate's flesh. Two more had passed through the muscle of his right arm. As he was cutting the last pellet from Slate's shoulder, Slate's yellow eyes slowly opened. Haines froze. Slate curled his mouth into something close to a smile, nodded once, and closed his eyes again.

❖ ❖ ❖

Poston crept through the wet forest, gun drawn. He was sure he was close to the gunfire site. The thrill of combat surged through him. He felt as if he were back on night patrols in 'Nam. He crept noiselessly through the brush and stopped when he saw a light to his left through the trees. He moved closer for a better view. In a small clearing he saw a lean-to made of a tarp and rough cut poles and under its cover he saw two men huddled over a figure on the ground. One of them held a six-volt lantern and the other held a combat knife. The man with the knife leaned back for a moment, and when Poston got a good look at the man on the ground, he almost cried out in surprise. Whatever was lying face up under the shelter was covered in dark fur, including its face. A chill ran through him. The tabloid picture was no fake. The monster was real.

He was so startled by the sight that he didn't hear the stealthy step behind him. A rifle butt crashed into the back of Poston's head and he fell face first, unconscious to the ground.

CHAPTER FORTY-NINE

"That's all we need," said Haines as Swede tied the warden's hands. "We can just leave him here," said Singer. "But he's seen us," said Haines, "and he's seen John as a werewolf."

At that moment Poston's radio crackled. "Poston, this is Simmons. We're at trail head sixteen B. Where the hell are you? Over."

"They're looking for him. That complicates things," said Haines. "Give me the goddamned radio." He keyed the handset and rubbed it back and forth against the bark of a pine tree.

"Say again, Elroy? All I'm getting is static. Over."

Haines uncapped a bottle from the first aid kit and poured peroxide into the mouthpiece. He keyed the handset and stuttered in a half whisper, "Ek. . .sig. . .mut . . .," and shut off the radio. "Bring a light over here." He spread the map on the ground and studied it for a moment. "Sixteen B is about six klicks north of here. There's another trailhead three clicks east. If we're lucky, we'll find a vehicle and beat it out of here before the Fish and Gamers send out a search party."

"What about these three?" Swede jerked his thumb at the dead mobsters. I don't think we have time for a funeral."

Haines shrugged and picked up Poston's Colt. He strode over to the dead men and fired two shots into each of them. "Untie the warden." Singer undid the ropes. Haines cocked the dart gun and fired it into Poston's thigh. He put the Colt in Poston's hand. "Problem solved. His buddies find him shot with a dart and six of his bullets in the dead guys. He won't come to for a while. By the time they sort it all out, we'll be far away. If he tells them he saw a werewolf, they'll write it off as a hallucination from the drugs in the dart. "

Swede grinned. "That's why we keep you on the payroll, Mikey. You think of everything. Let's get the hell out of here. I'll carry Johnny. You two can draw straws for Mandrake."

❖ ❖ ❖

Haines ran ahead to scout the trail head for vehicles. If they were lucky, they'd find something they could steal to drive out before the wardens found the crime scene and all hell broke loose. If they were really lucky, he'd find the Ford that belonged to the set of keys in one of the gangsters' pockets. Singer and Swede followed carrying the unconscious men. Leave no man behind, thought Haines, and tonight that applies to wizards and werewolves too.

He pushed through a dense thicket of laurel and in the trail head clearing before him stood a white Econoline van in the hazy moonlight. Lucky, lucky, lucky, he thought. Let's see how lucky. Fords had separate keys for the doors and the ignition. He tried the first of the two keys in the driver's door. No dice. He stuck the second key in the lock and turned it. The lock popped. Haines grinned. Let's see how long our luck lasts.

CHAPTER FIFTY

When the moon set, Slate transformed and when he was fully awake, he was largely healed but weak from the silver poisoning. He was lying in the back compartment of the armored van. Haines sat with his back propped against the compartment door, and between them Pegg lay bound and unconscious. Slate propped himself up on one elbow. The van rocked gently, and the hum of the tires told Slate they were on a paved road. "This van; I remember a white van with a cage that they used to move me around. I figure they brought it to take me back."

Haines nodded. "This is it. One of the dead guys had the keys in his pocket."

"They're all dead?"

"All but Mr. Wizard here. He'd be dead too, but you passed out about five seconds too soon. We thought it over and figured you deserved to take him out yourself."

Slate thought for a moment. "Their van and Pegg. Haines, you guys may not know it, but we just lucked into a perfect strike. I'm betting this van will be our ticket into Monzo's headquarters, especially with Pegg strapped into the passenger seat."

Survive.

Escape.

Payback.

CHAPTER FIFTY-ONE

Monzo sat behind his desk looking at the fading twilight over the New York skyline. He hadn't heard from Paco or Pegg for twenty-four hours. He had always been good at waiting, but the last month rubbed his nerves raw and wore his patience to a nub. Pegg had said, "Magic makes sinners of saints, let alone us lesser souls," but Brae's treachery still rankled him. Eddie was certain that he had killed Greystone and his henchman Smith in the fire, but Monzo would have felt better with bodies. And he lost two good men in the hit and a third, Leo's brother Sammy was barely alive. He was getting low on shooters, and there was always Stubbs waiting across Prospect to put his toe over the line.

Outside his office window the gathering gloom seemed a portent of things to come.

CHAPTER FIFTY-TWO

"So, the question is, do we go in before or after the moon comes up?" Haines stretched his legs in front of him and leaned his back against the rest stop picnic table.

"Either way, we have to go in while it's dark to get past the gate." Swede said. "Even with Mandrake there propped up in the passenger seat we might have a problem in the daylight."

Haines turned to Singer. "None of the mobsters have beards or mustaches, so you get to be the wheel man. But once we get inside the gate, we'll have to rush them before they see it's not one of their guys driving."

"As for before or after moonrise," said Singer, "I say we let our Fearless Leader make that call."

Slate raised his head from the table. "I'm about ninety percent healed from the silver, and the change may heal me the rest of the way or it may make me worse. I don't know. I'd ask Pegg, but he isn't talking at the moment." In the back of the van, Pegg lay unconscious. At the first sign he was waking, Haines shot him with a syringe of morphine. "When he comes to, there are plenty of things I need to ask him. If it was up to me, I'd take my chances as a werewolf, but it's not just for me to say. I kept control last night, but it's still a risky proposition."

"As if we never took risks before." said Swede.

Singer frowned. "What if they shoot you with silver again?"

"Then you'll just have to cut it out again. They'll expect me to come in as docile as a lamb because of Pegg. Once we're inside the fence, we can take the whole place down." He turned to Haines. "You have the amulet?"

Haines took it from his pocket and set it on the picnic table. The violet gemstone glowed and pulsed. "It looks intact. Singer hit Pegg's hand instead of the gadget."

"I think we ought to melt it down, or bury it, or something." Swede picked it up and turned it over in his hands.

Slate shook his head. "It's only a danger to us if Pegg has it. He knows how to use it. I don't, and destroying it may set off something worse that we can't control."

Singer nodded. "I can see that. So if we just keep it away from Pegg, we're okay?"

"Who knows?" said Slate. "I sure as hell don't. This whole magic business is a mine field."

"The Wizard knows," said Haines. "And maybe with the right persuasion he'll tell us."

"Or not," said Singer. "He could tell us any damned thing and we'd be none the wiser."

"Like I said before," said Slate, looking off into the distance. "Risky business."

CHAPTER FIFTY-TWO

Poston woke late in the afternoon between the clean white sheets of a hospital bed with Tom Barnet, his boss, and Ed Simmons sitting in chairs beside the bed. Neither of them looked as if he'd slept. He blinked the film out of his eyes and tried to sit up. He fell back onto the bed, his head spinning. "God, my mouth is dry. Tom, can you get me a drink?"

Barnett poured water from a carafe into a tumbler and put a straw in it. He held the glass while Poston took a long pull. "How you feeling, Elroy?"

"Like I have the world's worst hangover."

"I'm not surprised. The doctor said you got a hefty dose of horse tranquilizer from that dart." He lowered his voice. "Listen and listen good. There are two State Police detectives here, and you're lucky they went for coffee five minutes ago, or they'd be on you right now like flies on a turd. We got three bodies with your bullets in them. What the hell happened out there?"

Poston's head swam. He shook his head to clear it. "I didn't... don't..."

"You're in some deep shit, Elroy. You better think hard and remember before they get back here."

Poston closed his eyes and his head sank back on the pillow. Three dead bodies? He saw three people in the lean-to, no, two people and that thing on the ground. But then there had to be a fourth guy who slugged him. He felt the back of his head and found a painful lump at the base of his skull. He didn't imagine that part. Somebody must have gotten away. Did he come to and pull his Colt on them? A dart? Did they shoot him with a dart before he shot them, or was there a gun fight? He tried to think but images and ideas from a dozen times places floated between him and the night before.

"You called in 'shots fired,' Elroy," said Tom. "I told you to rendezvous with Simmons and Balzer and you acknowledged the order, but you didn't show up at sixteen B."

Simmons spoke up. "And a few minutes later we heard more shots. It took a while, but we found you with the dead guys."

The door opened and two men in off-the-rack suits came into the room. Poston smelled cops. The taller one with the oily hair said, "So he's awake now. Good. We have a few questions for you, Mr. Poston."

Barnett snapped, "For God's sake, Nichols, give him some time. He's just coming around."

Nichols grinned. "Maybe it's time for you two to go for coffee, Barnett."

"Like hell we will. That's my man and we're standing by him."

Parks, the shorter detective said, "Have it your way, Barnett. Just don't interfere." He pulled a small notebook and pen from an inside pocket, making sure Barnett saw the .38 in his armpit.

He shook his head to clear it.

"Mr. Poston." Nichols raised his voice. "Mr. Poston!"

Poston groaned. He couldn't play possum, but he could play sick. "What…who?"

"I'm detective Nichols and this is detective Parks. We're with the New Jersey State Police Organized Crime Task Force. You had quite a night. Tell us about it."

Organized crime? "I don't remember," Poston half whispered.

"Maybe these will help." Parks held up a handful of Polaroid photos. One by one he held them in front of Poston's face. They were full body shots and face close-ups of three men, three dead men. He recognized two of them as two of the men with Hanisford, the photographer. The third was missing most of his face.

"Do you recognize these men, Mr. Poston?" Nichols said, "Because we do. They're all members of the Monzo crime family. We confirmed their IDs this afternoon; Paul Guccione, Leo Taglia, and James Pacone. These guys sure as hell weren't tourists or hunters. We want to know what they were doing there after dark and why you shot them."

Parks chimed in, "You reported a large patch of marijuana growing in the Barrens a few days ago. You said you suspected it belonged to the Tuttle brothers. Do you think it's just a coincidence that those three rednecks turned up dead the same week as three drug dealing mobsters?"

"Now wait a minute," growled Barnett. "You're not trying to tie him in with some drug operation."

Nichols turned a cold stare on Barnett. "Give us credit for some smarts, will you. It all adds up. Say the Tuttles were growing weed for Monzo. Suddenly they end up dead and a week later Elroy here reports the weed patch. A week or so goes by and three of Monzo's people show up in the middle of the goddamned wilderness in the middle of the night to find out what's what. And who comes to the party? Elroy Poston. The guns come out but they overlook the fact that Elroy is an ex Army Ranger, not your average game warden, no offense, and he takes them all down."

"Hold it right there." Barnett spat the words through clenched teeth. "If he was in on it, why did he report the marijuana patch?"

"Because he had to," sneered Parks. "That hunter who got his foot blown off called attention to the place. He had to call it in to cover his involvement."

"That's a load of horseshit," groaned Poston. "I don't know anything about this."

"Shut up, Elroy," Barnett hissed. "Don't say another goddamned word 'til we get you a lawyer."

"He doesn't need an attorney," snapped Nichols. "We aren't arresting him or even charging him with anything."

Barnett jumped up and put a finger in Nichols' face. "You boys aren't the only ones who know about Miranda rights. We got the same seminar on it you did. This man was acting under my supervision in his official capacity as a game warden, and right now he's in no condition to be given the third degree by a couple of dickheads; no offense."

Parks snapped his notebook shut. "You're making a big mistake, Barnett."

"Maybe I am, and maybe not. You'll get my report as soon as I can type it up, seeing as I don't have a secretary."

Nichols glared at him. "This isn't over by a long stretch, Barnett. Count on that." He leered down at Poston. "Congratulations, Elroy. You killed Michael Monzo's cousin and chief lieutenant. You're going to need us to protect you, pal. If I were you, I'd think long and hard about cooperating." The detectives stalked out of the room, slamming the door behind them.

Poston raised his head. "Thanks, Tom."

"Don't thank me yet, Elroy. By the time I'm done looking at this, you'll think those two are the frigging Hardy Boys."

Barnett and Simmons sat back down. Poston's last thought before he slipped back into dreamland was, "Deep shit" is an understatement.

CHAPTER FIFTY-THREE

"Too bad about the Ranger," said Swede.

"You mean the game warden?" said Singer.

"No, I mean the Ranger. He was wearing an Army Ranger's ring. He was one of us."

"Yeah," chimed in Haines, "back when you were one of them. I wouldn't worry about him too much. The autopsies on those gorillas will show he didn't kill anybody. They were already dead when they were shot with the Colt. And if they did a paraffin test on him, they'll realize he never fired the weapon. He'll twist in the wind for a few days, but he'll walk away from it in one piece. He's getting off easy. Those gangsters would have killed him without thinking twice about it."

"I get the feeling he'd've taken them with him," said Swede.

"Probably so," said Haines and leaned back in the passenger seat, closing his eyes and the conversation.

The van rolled up I-95 at a steady sixty miles per hour. They'd be in Newark in another ninety minutes, the moon would rise in three hours, and then the show would begin.

CHAPTER FIFTY-FOUR

The last evening light was fading and Manhattan's skyline glowed in the distance. Monzo sat staring out the window of his office. The longer he waited for Paco or Pegg to contact him, the more worried he became. Twenty four hours had passed since he had heard from either one of them. Something must be desperately wrong. There was a knock at the door. "Yeah?"

Eddie put his head inside the door. "Mike, there's a call for you. It's Amos Whelker's assistant, Frye."

Monzo's head snapped up. "What does he want?"

Eddie shook his head. "He wouldn't say, just that it was important that he talk to you right away."

"Okay, Eddie, I'll handle it." Eddie nodded and pulled a chair over to the desk.

Monzo stared at the phone on his desk. One of its buttons winked off and on. Direct contact like this was a complete breach of protocol. Whelker's people must be crazy to call me directly, he thought. Either that or something drastic has happened. He picked up the handset. "This is Michael Monzo."

"This is Robert Frye, Mr. Monzo. Mr. Whelker asked that I call you because we couldn't reach Mr. Brae."

"Whatever this is, it damned well better be important."

"I'm afraid it is, sir. The State Police are trying to keep a lid on this information, but an inside source of ours just told us that three of your people were killed in a shootout last night in the Pine Barrens. One of them was your cousin Paco."

Monzo held the phone away from his ear and stared at it as if it were a snake. From the earpiece he heard Frye's tinny voice: "Mr. Monzo? Mr. Monzo?"

Monzo took a deep breath and picked up the handset. "Yes," he said in a toneless voice. "I'm here. Who are the other two?"

"Leo Taglia and Paul Guccione."

"How did this happen?"

"We don't have many details. It seems a game warden shot them all when they fired at him."

"And who is this warden?"

"I'm afraid we don't know that yet."

"I want that name. Do you understand? You find out. And when you do, you tell me first."

"Yes sir. I understand. And Mr. Monzo…"

"Yeah?"

"Mr. Whelker sends his condolences."

Monzo slammed the phone down so hard the earpiece broke off the handset and landed halfway across the room. Eddie stared.

Monzo raised his eyes to meet Eddie's. "I don't know how it all happened, but Paco is dead, Paul and Leo are dead. No mention of Pegg. That means that bastard is still alive somewhere."

Eddie's eyes blazed. "I'll bet he used his mumbo-jumbo to save his own hide." His hands curled into fists.

"Either that or he set us up. Either way, we're going to find Pegg and when we do, we'll make him pay to square things for Paco." Monzo sat silent for a moment then roared and slammed his fists on the desktop. In the back of his mind, Monzo thought that maybe Pegg wasn't at fault, but anger pushed the idea away.

"Blood for blood, Mike," Eddie said solemnly. "Blood for Blood."

Monzo opened the desk drawer and pulled out a cleaver. He looked himself in the eye of his reflection in its blade and ran his thumb along its edge. "That's right, Eddie. Blood for blood."

CHAPTER FIFTY-FIVE

Two miles from the factory, the team prepped for the operation. Pegg was still out from the morphine, so Swede and Singer tied him to the passenger seat. Slate found Pegg's tinted glasses in a coat pocket and put them on his nose. "That way, they won't see his eyes are shut." They had wadded gauze and stuffed it into his mouth to keep him from mouthing a spell, but Slate wasn't sure the wizard still didn't have some cards left to play.

"Because the van doors can only be opened from the outside, Haines and Swede, you'll have to hold them shut and unlatched from the inside. When the play goes down, open them up. Swede, you take the back, Haines, you take the side. Because they're steel reinforced, they'll be good shields. Monzo had two hitters on the door the night I got away, so we should expect at least two outside. I can't guess what muscle he might have in the building. You guys clear the entrance. I'll go in after Monzo, and you follow me with Pegg in case we need him as a bargaining chip. Inside, shoot anything that moves, and I do mean 'thing.' Who knows what else Pegg may have cooked up for Monzo since I escaped. We on it?"

Heads nodded all around. Slate looked up at the sky. "Any minute now."

CHAPTER FIFTY-SIX
MOONRISE.

Frankie and Ron stood guard outside the factory. Something was up besides the moon, and it was something big. Frankie always knew when Eddie was upset, everybody knew, but Frankie had a sixth sense about the Boss. Something bad had happened after the Boss wasted Brae; Frankie wished he knew what it was. He hated working blind, but the Boss would tell them when he was ready.

"Hey, somebody's coming," Ron said around his cigarette. Frankie checked his shotgun, a little jealous that Ron got the fancy Army gun, but Ron used an M-16 when he got drafted, so Eddie gave it to him. Lights pulled up to the gate. Ron strained his eyes. "It's the van. Pegg's in the front seat. Open the gate."

Frankie threw the switch and the chain link gate jangled aside. The van rolled in, but as it got closer, instead of slowing, it sped up, aimed straight for the front door. "What the hell?" yelled Ron, his cigarette falling from his mouth. Blinded by the headlights, he hesitated but instinct took over. He raised the M-16 and sprayed a burst of fire into the front of the van.

Singer wrenched the wheel hard right and slammed on the brakes. The van slid sideways and as it did, the cargo door slid back and Haines opened fire, an automatic in each hand. Frankie's thick torso was an easy target, and the slugs ripped through him as he pulled the shotgun around and fired. Ron was frantically ramming a fresh magazine into the M-16 when Swede opened up from behind the back door, giving him two blasts full on from the Ithaca.

Slate leapt from the cargo door and landed on the balls of his feet. He howled in rage and charged the entry door, knocking it from its hinges and ran headlong into the darkened building. Haines started for the door after him and said over his shoulder to Singer, "Bring Pegg and follow us."

Singer opened the driver's and slid out covered with broken glass from the shattered windshield and with a hand over his bleeding shoulder. "Got some bad news." He jerked his head toward the passenger seat. Pegg sat still upright, tied to the seat, but his dark glasses were askew, the left lens shattered. A rivulet of blood trickled from his eye socket where a slug from the M-16 had passed through on its way into his skull.

"Damn," said Haines. "So much for hostages."

Swede crouched over Ron's body. "Well, I'll be damned." He dropped the Ithaca and picked up the M-16. "Just like old times." He stood and ran after Haines into the factory.

Because he'd lost so many men Monzo had only a skeleton crew manning the building. They came running at the sound of gunfire. The first to burst into the entrance corridor was met with a disemboweling slash of Slate's claws. The others ran past his quivering, screaming body and chased Slate down the corridor as he ran for the second-floor stairs. The mobsters opened fire at the werewolf and in an instant two of them fell as Swede and Haines fired from behind. The gunfight was on from opposing ends of the dark hallway.

Haines crouched in a doorway to the left. Swede was hunkered down to the right behind a crate. "I count five," said Swede. "You take the two on the right and I'll take the three on the left." Swede held an automatic at arm's length to his left and fired down the corridor. "Immediately, flashes erupted from the mobsters' guns in response. Swede let loose with a burst from the M-16 and heard a scream. One down. Haines fired both hands at the muzzle flashes and saw the flash of a machine gun firing into the ceiling as a dying man pulled the trigger in a death grip. That's two, he thought. Let's just hope he didn't hit Slate overhead through the floor.

Slate bounded up the stairs, three and four at a time. He burst through the outer door of Monzo's office suite as the gunfire echoed through the building. He leapt over a desk and threw himself into the closed door of the inner office. It swung inward on an empty room. The lights were on, but no one was there. Below, the gunfire stopped.

Slate howled in fury as he raced from room to room, all empty. Monzo was gone.

A sound behind him. He whirled to find Swede and Haines in the empty hallway. He smelled blood and death. His head spun. He dropped into a crouch, snarling.

"John," said Haines, "it's us, your team. Focus, man." One hand reached into his pocket and pulled out the amulet. The other hand slipped slowly under his jacket where he'd hidden an automatic with silver bullets he took from one of the dead mobsters in the Barrens. Haines held the amulet high in front of him. "Focus."

Immediately Slate froze, transfixed by the glowing gem. Focus. Images and thoughts whirled through Slate's mind, and he seized one like a drowning man grabs a stick of wood: the stone figure, distant at first, but he dragged it closer to him, wrapped his consciousness around it, and slowly, calm returned. He straightened from his crouch and raised his right paw. The elongated fingers curled inward into a fist, and a grotesque clawed thumb pointed upward.

Haines let out a long-held breath. "Let's get out of here, John. We'll get him next time."

Slate took one last look around him, nodded, and bounded down the stairs.

CHAPTER FIFTY-SEVEN

Monzo sat behind his desk at The Cricket. A game warden. He pounded the desk. A goddamned game warden! The door opened and Eddie came in along with a blast of noise. Outside on the dance floor, music blared, people laughed, and the club was in full swing. He'd come to The Cricket to think, finding the silence of the factory maddening, but he found the raucous noise of the club just as distracting. Eddie set the bottle of scotch on Monzo's desk and put down two glasses. "Have a drink, Mike," he said. "I know I need one." He poured three fingers of scotch in both glasses.

Eddie picked up his glass and Monzo stared at his own. He hesitated for a few seconds then picked his up and clinked against Eddie's. "To Paco. As soon as we find out the name of that game warden, he's gonna find out it's open season big time."

"I'll drink to that." Eddie downed his in one pull.

A blast of noise made both look to the door. It swung shut and standing before them were two men in dark suits, one a gangly hunchbacked man with a crooked grin and the other a tall cadaverous man with a face that looked as if it were carved from marble.

"Who the hell are you? How'd you get past security?" Eddie reached into his coat, but before his piece cleared the holster, The Whisperer held up his hand, palm open. His lips moved and his fingers slowly curled inward. Eddie's eyes bulged and he clutched at his chest, gasping for breath. The Whisperer's hand closed into a fist, crushing Eddie's heart and crushing out his life. Eddie fell dead to the floor.

He turned his eyes to Monzo, who had risen from his chair. "Mr. Monzo, allow me to introduce myself. My name is Greystone."

Monzo's hand darted for the panic button under the desktop, but as quick as a panther, Smith reached across the desk and caught his hand in an iron grip. Monzo swung his left in a hard hook that caught Smith just under his eye. Smith cried out in pain and fell back, the sigil on his hand smoldering from Monzo's ring. The ring had opened Smith's skin and it hung like a leather flap almost to his jaw line.

"A gift from our mutual acquaintance Mr. Pegg, no doubt," said the Whisperer." His smile was more frightening than his voice. "Two can play that game, Mr. Monzo." His lips moved, and the ring began to glow, red, then yellow, then white, searing Monzo's flesh. He clawed it off, singeing his fingertips as he did. The ring fell to the desk where it branded a perfect circle into the wood.

"You have been a distraction to me, Mr. Monzo, and you have placed yourself between me and my objectives. You will distract me no more. The Whisperer pointed both index fingers at Monzo and mouthed words that only he could hear. Monzo's lips pulled back from his teeth and further. He clutched at them with his hands, trying to hold them together, but they gaped wider and wider still with a wet ripping sound as his skin tore loose from his flesh. The lips pulled further apart taking his nose and chin with them, leaving a gory mask of raw bone and muscle with eyes that would never close again. The human rind peeled over his head and down below his collarbone into the white shirt that rapidly turned scarlet with hot fresh blood. The force of the separating skin burst the seams of Monzo's clothing and it fell around him in bloody rags.

Monzo screamed in pain and terror as his legs peeled away. He staggered through the office door and onto the dance floor where he writhed in a grotesque reel to the raucous music as the terrified crowd ran in panic. By ones and twos the band stopped playing as they saw him, dropped their instruments and joined the mad rush for the door. The weaker fell before the mob and were trampled while others were crushed against the walls of the entrance.

The Whisperer stood on the edge of the dance floor watching Monzo die. He nodded to Mr. Smith who stepped behind the bar. The hunchback poured two bottles of brandy on the curtains behind the bandstand and lit a match from a book left on one of the tables. In a moment, The Cricket was ablaze and the flames were racing toward the crush of screaming patrons. Firelight sparkled on the wet red gloss of Monzo's corpse as it shuddered its last.

The Whisperer raised his eyes to the ceiling as if reading words written above.

> *"And on the pedestal these words appear:*
> *'My name is Ozymandias, King of Kings:*
> *Look on my works, ye mighty, and despair!'*
> *Nothing beside remains. Round the decay*
> *Of that colossal wreck, boundless and bare,*
> *the lone and level sands stretch far away."*

The Whisperer nodded in satisfaction, turned and walked away with Mr. Smith in tow.

CHAPTER FIFTY-EIGHT

In a motel room outside Philadelphia, the team listened as Haines read the third newspaper account of the night before. "'In what appears to be a new chapter in a gang war for the domination of Newark, a gun battle in an abandoned factory building left nine men dead, all apparent minions of reputed crime boss Michael Monzo. Almost simultaneously Monzo and his brother Edward died in a mysterious fire at Monzo's newly acquired Newark nightclub The Cricket that has also killed at least twenty-five patrons. These deaths follow those the day before of three of Monzo's employees in a shootout in a remote area of the Pine Barrens.

"'Police Commissioner Amos Whelker says that these deaths "cannot be coincidence," and that he is bringing the full power of the Newark Police Department to bear on the investigation in conjunction with the State Police Organized Crime Task Force and the Federal Bureau of Investigation. "We will not allow gangs to run this town," Whelker says.' Shall I go on?"

"Seems they all say the same thing," said Singer.

"Yeah," said Slate. "Pegg's dead. And so is Monzo."

"So, does that wrap it up?" said Swede, throwing a beer can at the wastebasket and missing by a good six inches.

"Somewhere out there is whoever sicced the first werewolf, Pegg called him Kovacks, on the gang. I don't know if he's after me or not. If he is, he's got magic on his side. And if he's got one of those," he pointed to the amulet where it glowed on the table, "He'll have me by the nuts. And you've seen what can happen. I'm guessing it'll get worse. I don't expect you three to hang around and be exposed to that kind of risk."

"We can decide that later," Haines put in. "We're going to babysit you or two more nights. We can't just walk off and leave you on a rampage all over the countryside."

"We found a safe quiet place for you to stay for the next two nights where you can change and not hurt anybody," said Swede.

"If I can change without going wild for two more nights, I can probably manage on my own."

"We'll see," said Haines, "and in two days we'll make some decisions."

CHAPTER FIFTY-NINE

B arnett came to Poston's room the next day as he was dressing. He'd be discharged in a few minutes as soon as the doctor signed the papers. He'd suffered no lasting effect from the tranquilizer, but that was small comfort in the face of the shitstorm that was headed his way.

"Seen today's paper, Elroy?" Barnett wasn't smiling, but he wasn't frowning either. Poston shook his head.

"Big news in Newark. That crime boss Monzo that Nichols and Parks were so hot for died last night in a night club fire, and at the same time a bunch of his boys got shot up at his hideout. The state boys were barking up my ass pretty hard for a day then all of a sudden things got quiet. I guess Newark's a bigger deal."

Poston buttoned his shirt. "Is that good?"

"Good for me. I didn't look forward to going head to head with those two, though I would have and I still will if it comes to that. And it still may. Nichols and Parks wanted your badge and your head big time. But it's good for you that the gang is pretty well wiped out. I don't think they'll come looking for you any time soon, either. I went to the autopsies. The good news is it seems all three of those men were dead before you shot them, so you're clear on that charge. The bad news is that opens a big bag of questions that I can't answer."

At that moment, the nurse came in with a clipboard full of discharge papers. Poston signed them all and as she left, Barnett quietly closed the door and stood between it and Poston, his arms folded. "You're a good warden, Elroy, and I believe you're a good man to boot. And serving your country stands for something, too, but I have to suspend you pending the official inquiry. You can tell me the story now, man to man, and I'll help you all I can, or you can wait for the board, and it's out of my hands."

Poston looked him square in the eyes. "I don't remember, Tom, and that's the truth."

Barnett nodded and stepped away from the door. "So be it."

Poston was almost through the door when Barnett called after him. "By the way, I hear one of those mobsters' guns was full of silver bullets. What was that all about?"

Poston turned and looked Barnett square in the eye. "I don't know, Tom." And as he walked down the corridor, he thought, *but if takes me the rest of my life, I'm going to find out.*

CHAPTER SIXTY

Behind a desk in Langley, Virginia, Carlton Briggs ground out a cigarette as he stared at a picture. It was the sketch-artist face of a dark-haired man with a moustache, longish hair, and a scar that divided his eyebrow in two. The sketch had been circulated around New Jersey and New York by underworld types looking for its subject. It could be Slate, but even if it were not, this man had to be found to be certain. He picked up the phone and punched the intercom for his aide. "Get the director for me. I expect he'll be at home by now." *Slate,* he thought, *why the hell can't you stay dead?*

CHAPTER SIXTY-ONE

Slate sat in a chair for the second night in the huge freezer of the defunct meat packing plant outside Willow Hill. It was a really good place for him to change, even if it was a little claustrophobic. The change had come and for the second night he had stayed still. He was able to think, free of distraction in the featureless room, and he felt a sense of total control. This must be what Kovacks, the werewolf he'd killed, had learned to do, to coexist with the beast and subdue it with reason. If he was careful, he could work with the change and keep a rein on the killing urge.

Pegg's death was a mixed bag. There was a lot that Slate could have learned from the wizard, but keeping him around would have been like carrying a rattlesnake in his pocket. There was so much to find out, and he would have to work hard to do it.

He heard the clank of the heavy door latch. Slate's yellow eyes narrowed and he leaned forward in the chair, ready to spring. The door swung open and the team came in. They hung back, a little hesitant. Haines stepped forward, hands out palms up.

"Do you understand me, John?" said Haines. "Do you know what I'm saying?" Slate hesitated, as if translating the words then nodded. "We've talked it all over and reasoned out a few things. We were careful, but I know some of our prints are bound to show up at one hit scene or another, and sooner or later they'll land on some desk under the sidewalk in D.C. And once the Company knows we're still breathing and we're a threat to their existence, they'll be coming after us. We want to take it to them, and to do that, we'll need an edge."

One by one, each man rolled up a sleeve. They formed a close semicircle around Slate's chair and held out their arms.

Swede chuckled. "You know, I never thought I'd ever say this to you, Johnny. Bite me."

Survive.

Escape.

Payback.

Hitwolf.

THE END

ABOUT OUR CREATORS

WRITER –

FRED ADAMS JR. is a western Pennsylvania native who has enjoyed a lifelong love affair with horror, fantasy, and science fiction literature and films. He holds a Ph.D. in American Literature from Duquesne University and recently retired from teaching writing and literature in the English Department of Penn State University.

He has published over 50 short stories in amateur, and professional magazines as well as hundreds of news features as a staff writer and sportswriter for the now Pittsburgh Tribune-Review. In the 1970s Fred published the fanzine Spoor and its companion The Spoor Antholoyg. His novel, Hitwolf, which will see print in early 2014 from Airship 27 is his first, and his nonfiction book, Edith Wharton's American Gothic: Gods, Ghosts, and Vampires will be published by Borgo Press in 2014.

INTERIOR ILLUSTRATOR –

CLAYTON HINKLE is a life-long, self taught (for the most part) artist whose main ambition in life is to draw cool, adventurous, fantastic, horror-ific Pulp and Comic art. Most, if not all, of his published work has been in the New Pulp field, Airship 27 Productions being the major outlet of his wares by far, as well as work for the fanzine "REH, Two-Gun Raconteur," a 'zine dedicated to the late, great Robert E. Howard and his works. Clayton hopes to one day make his living by drawing, pure and simple.

COVER ARTIST –

INGRID HARDY has a life-long passion for drawing, and a faithful love of horses, reading and conspiracy, and has been busy drawing for many years. She contributes illustrations on an ongoing basis to a Quebec-based horse magazine, and as a Lucas Film approved artist, has worked on sketch cards sets for Topps such as Star Wars 30th Anniversary, several Indiana Jones sets, Star Wars Clone Wars, Star Wars Galaxy 4 as well as Lord of the Rings Masterpieces 2, Heroes volumes 1 and 2, not to mention, many personally commissioned sketch cards and small paintings. She is always looking for something new to try. You can visit her website at: (www.vikingillus.com). She lives with her husband, Michel, two kids, a fuzzy black cat and a sausage dog.

The Return of RAVENWOOD

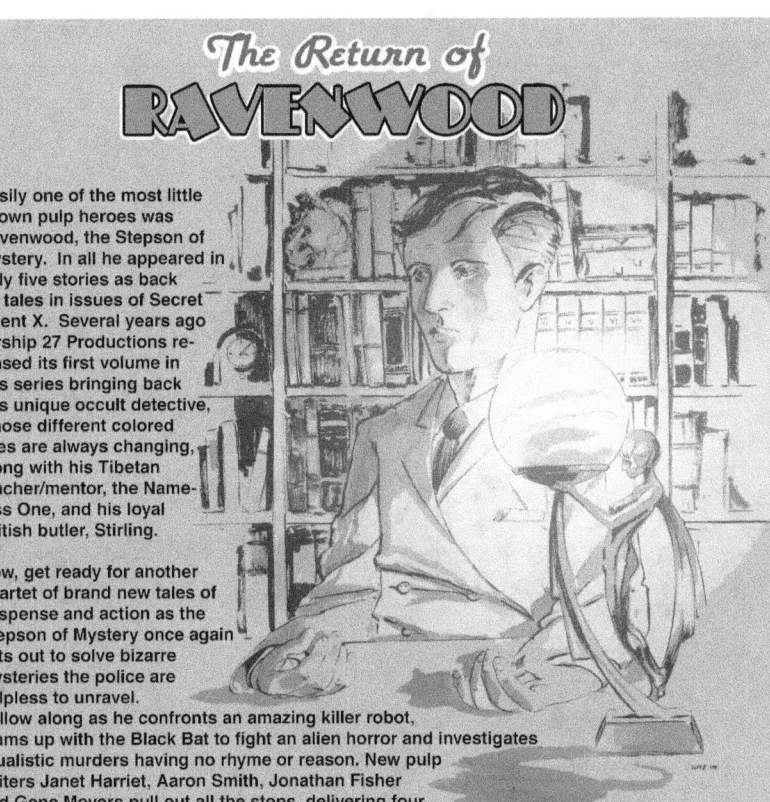

Easily one of the most little known pulp heroes was Ravenwood, the Stepson of Mystery. In all he appeared in only five stories as back up tales in issues of Secret Agent X. Several years ago Airship 27 Productions released its first volume in this series bringing back this unique occult detective, whose different colored eyes are always changing, along with his Tibetan teacher/mentor, the Nameless One, and his loyal British butler, Stirling.

Now, get ready for another quartet of brand new tales of suspense and action as the Stepson of Mystery once again sets out to solve bizarre mysteries the police are helpless to unravel. Follow along as he confronts an amazing killer robot, teams up with the Black Bat to fight an alien horror and investigates ritualistic murders having no rhyme or reason. New pulp writers Janet Harriet, Aaron Smith, Jonathan Fisher and Gene Moyers pull out all the stops, delivering four original, fast-paced adventures that skirt the outer edges of fear and madness.

This is one pulp book best read with the lights on!

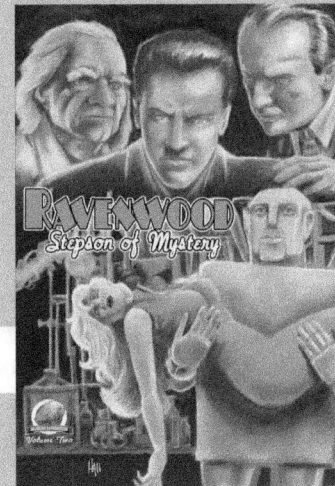

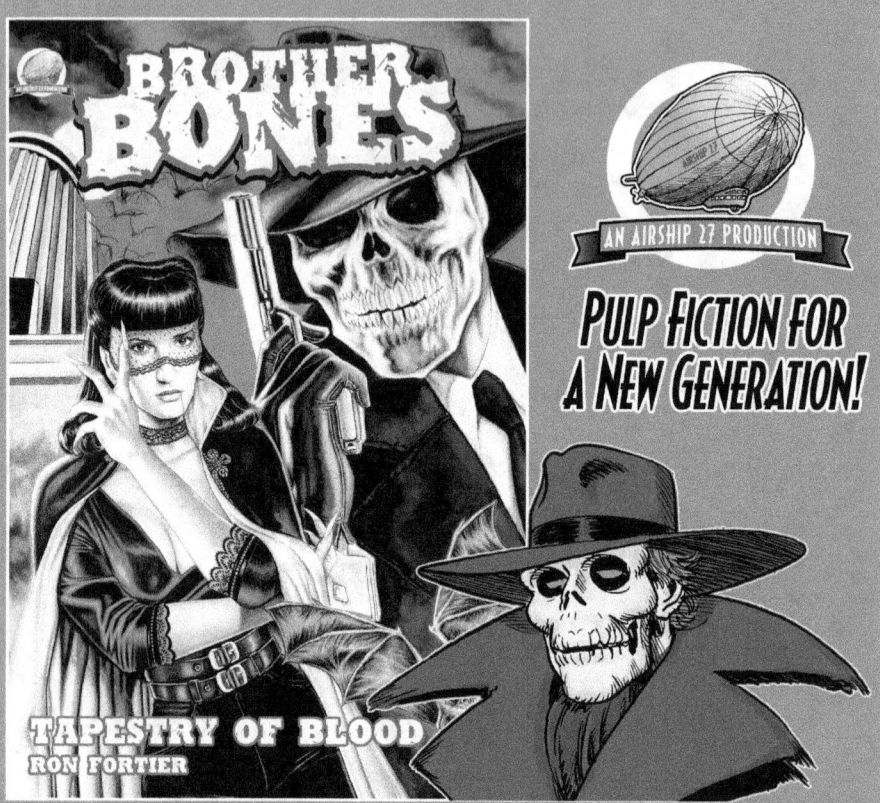

www.ingramcontent.com/pod-product-compliance
Lightning Source LLC
Chambersburg PA
CBHW071242250626
47163CB00001B/291